BLOOD TIES

A JUNKYARD DRUID URBAN FANTASY SHORT
STORY COLLECTION

M.D. MASSEY

MODERN DIGITAL PUBLISHING

NOTE TO READERS

The events in *Old Ghosts* occur immediately after Book Five in *The Colin McCool Paranormal Suspense Series*. Events in *The Goblin King* occur concurrently with events in Book Six of the series, and Hemi's story in *Going Under* happens sometime between Books Five and Six.

Thus, here lie spoilers... you have been warned.

Certainly, these stories can be enjoyed as standalones, if you don't wish to read the rest of the novels first.

But for those who are so inclined, here's a chronological reading order for books I've released in the Colin McCool universe to date:

- *Druid Blood*
- *Blood Scent*
- *Junkyard Druid*
- *Graveyard Druid*
- *Moonlight Druid*
- *Underground Druid*

- *Blood Circus*
- *Druid Justice*
- *Blood Ties*
- *Druid Enforcer*

You may also wish to read my *THEM Post-Apocalyptic Series*, as Colin makes appearances in Books Three and Five. However, you don't need to read those novels to know what's going on in Colin's world.

OLD GHOSTS

In which Colin discovers a gift from a Celtic god is a mixed blessing.

1

The rumbling beneath my feet intensified, shaking the nearby stacks of junked cars until they swayed and threatened to topple over on me. I had no idea what sort of magic I'd unleashed by planting the Dagda's acorn, but I knew enough to get the hell out of the way of several tons of falling metal. Backing away, I narrowly avoided being crushed by a seventies-era Lincoln Continental with a smashed front end.

The earthquake caused by the acorn's fae magic seemed to be localized to within about twenty yards of the site where I'd planted it. Once I escaped the immediate area, I could safely observe the results of my decision to plant a tree in memory of Elmo, the gentle ogre who'd died at the hands of Commander Gunnarson and his thugs on that very spot. I still blamed myself for his death as well as Uncle Ed's, neglectful as I'd been in protecting them from my enemies. But what was done was done, and nothing I did was going to bring them back.

Not unless the Dagda's magic acorn could raise the dead.

Pfft. Fat chance of that.

Yet something mysterious and dangerous *was* happening now that I'd planted it, that much was clear. The ground continued to shake, and cars toppled and fell until a large pile of automobile husks covered the spot where I'd buried the acorn. *Is the seed reacting to Elmo's remains?* I wondered. *Or is it simply supposed to respond this way after being planted?*

I guessed the latter. There had to be a very good reason why the Dagda had given me the thing in the first place. He was the deity who'd first taught druidry to the Celts, and I suspected he didn't want our order to die out. As to why, I had no idea.

One thing I'd learned in my interactions with gods and demigods was that their motives were often difficult to fathom. Whether due to boredom, capriciousness, or madness caused by near-immortality, they seemed to delight in meddling with the lives of humankind. Finnegas, my mentor in all things druidic, had taught me that none of the fae or *Tuatha de Danann* could be trusted —not even the ones who seemed benign and friendly.

As Finn had taught me, and as I'd observed time and again in my dealings with them, they were all of an alien mind and possessed of motives that mere mortals could not fathom. While the acorn had been a gift from the Dagda, who seemed to be the kindest deity in all the Celtic pantheon, I was certain he had an ulterior motive for giving it to me. Exhibit A: I might have easily been killed by the magic released when the acorn was planted. But had the Dagda bothered to warn me? Nope. He'd just given me the damned thing and told me not to lose it.

What a dick. We were definitely going to have words the next time I saw him. Which, I expected, wouldn't be far off. The gods, petty as they were, had a tendency to return to the scenes of their crimes. Sure as the sun would rise tomorrow, the Dagda would be along eventually to check out his handiwork.

Speaking of which, the rumbling and ground tremors were beginning to subside. Curious as to what might come next, I took a few cautious steps toward the pile of junked cars that had covered Elmo's burial site. Pausing at a distance I deemed safe, I dropped to the ground and planted an ear to the earth. *Silence.*

I wasn't convinced the spell's effects were over, so I stayed put and continued to listen. After a few minutes had passed, I decided to probe the burial spot with my druid senses to determine what was happening down there. I dropped into a druid trance, slowing my breathing and extending my senses—first to the area directly under the piled cars, then deeper into the earth.

There. I sensed something alive—not an animal life form, but something plant-like. And I did mean "plant-like," since this was unlike anything I'd encountered before. How I'd not felt it before when I'd held the acorn was a mystery to me. The raw magical power it held now very nearly overwhelmed my druidic senses.

From what I could tell, the acorn had burrowed deeper into the soil, a good six feet or more beneath where I'd planted it. Now, the thing pulsed with life, energy, and magic, like a heart beating deep within the soil. But something was missing. In fact, it seemed as though the little acorn was waiting for something, some kind of trigger or signal.

Don't do it, McCool.

Ignoring my better judgement, I reached out toward the seed with my senses, probing it with my mind to determine its purpose and current disposition. Would it cause more tremors, or was it now dormant again? I needed to know, because if the junkyard employees were in danger, I'd have to shut our operations down until I found a way to contain it. The last thing I needed was for some poor soul to get crushed under a bunch of cars or sucked into a sinkhole in the middle of the yard.

I cautiously expanded my awareness closer to the seed, examining it from all angles. Thus far, the shell hadn't cracked. That was good news. Maybe if I left it alone, it'd revert back to an inert state. I decided I'd need to ward it, or rather ward the dirt around it, to prevent anyone from accidentally messing with it. The chances of someone digging here were almost nil, and the twenty tons or so of junked cars lying atop it would help dissuade anyone from trying. But eventually, we'd have to move the pile of scrap. That meant there'd be nothing between the Dagda's spellwork and our employees and customers but a few feet of dirt. Fae magic was tricky, which was why I didn't want to risk it.

I sent my magic out toward the acorn, intending to compact and harden the earth around it—then I'd cast a compulsion that would discourage anyone from digging there. Just a tiny little spell was all it'd take, enough to protect the acorn and keep anyone from digging it up again...

As soon as my magic touched the acorn, I knew I'd messed up. The rumbling that had toppled the cars earlier recommenced even more violently, and the seed's outer shell popped open with a loud *crack* that was audible aboveground. An instant later, I sensed rather than saw a small green shoot breaking free from within the seed as magic began to pulse in waves from its center.

Too late, I scrambled to my feet. I took a few stumbling steps before the earth liquified like quicksand underfoot, pulling me in up to my waist and preventing my escape.

2

Soil liquefaction was a phenomenon that often occurred during earthquakes, and I knew liquified soil could swallow cars and topple buildings. But central Texas dirt was full of clay, which prevented natural soil liquefaction. So, I knew that what I was experiencing had more to do with magic forces involved than it did the earthquake.

I fought to free myself from the soil, but it was like swimming in cake batter. Pressing on the ground's surface only resulted in sinking my hands and forearms into the dirt, putting me in danger of being completely engulfed. I considered shifting into my Fomorian form to free myself, but quickly decided against it. This was Tuatha magic, after all, and the Fomoire had once been their mortal enemies. There was no telling how the spell might react to the presence of a Fomorian creature in its midst. I decided to just relax and wait for the spell to end. Then, if I was still alive and not totally submerged in liquid earth, I could find a way to dig myself free.

At least, that's what I planned before the ground started moving.

Earlier, all I'd noticed was a lot of shaking. The surface of the earth beneath me had pretty much stayed in place. But now, the ground was starting to move in a circular pattern along with everything on top of it—first slowly, then with ever-increasing speed. Doing my best to ride on top of the liquified soil, I looked around to determine exactly what was going on.

Realization hit me like a ton of bricks. *It's a freaking whirlpool—the ground is turning into a whirlpool of dirt.*

As the earth churned, gravity and inertia pulled its contents—dirt, rocks, and about twenty tons of junked cars and parts in varying states of decay—toward the center of the whirlpool. And me too, of course—although I was frantically trying to extricate myself from what might become my very own strange, magical grave.

Elmo, buddy... I just might be joining you soon.

Unable to free myself from the whirlpool's pull, I instead examined the center of the swirling mass of earth, stone, and metal in the magical spectrum. Soon, all became clear. Beneath the earth's surface, the sprout that had only moments ago been nothing more than a tiny, fragile tree shoot was now growing at a phenomenal pace.

Magic no longer pulsed from the thing, but instead swirled around the seedling—much in the same way a rotating black hole spun in a vortex that threatened to suck everything into it. With each revolution, nutrients were pulled out of the soil to feed the growing shoot. Rocks smashed against one another, crushed by the magic to extract valuable minerals needed for the tree's growth. Like a small, green singularity, the spell I'd released was converting earth, stone, and metal into plant matter at an unbelievable pace.

Clouds began to gather overhead—dark grey thunderheads that rolled in seemingly from nowhere and everywhere at once. I smelled ozone as thunder rumbled in the sky above, then rain began to fall in fat, wet drops that drenched me and soaked the ground, turning the swirling soil to liquid mud. The rain increased in intensity for some time, and seconds passed into minutes as I remained caught in nature's carnival ride from hell. I had no idea if the spell had been designed to save unwary druids from drowning in a maelstrom of earth and mud, or if I was just lucky to not have been sucked under yet. I just wished the damned thing would stop.

Finally, the clouds parted and sunlight touched the whirlpool of mud once more. At the center, car parts and rocks dissolved as if made of sugar while the ground roiled and spun around that central axis, clearing a space roughly five feet across. I watched, stupefied and somewhat motion sick, as a sapling shot up from the earth in the now empty space at the center of the magical turbulence.

All the while, I was being pulled toward the center, along with all the solid matter that was being "digested" to feed the sapling's growth. The tree took only seconds to expand in girth and height to the size of a five-year-old oak. Moments later, even more earth and minerals had been sucked into the center of the spell, feeding the tree as it rapidly matured.

Roots spread from the trunk, which continued to increase in size as branches and leaves sprouted everywhere above—until a vast canopy of green extended outward, obscuring the sky. And still the ground spun around the tree, and I with it, even though the spell had by now sucked every last piece of metal either underground or into the tree to fuel its accelerated growth.

I estimated the tree's trunk to now be three or four feet across. Although I couldn't see how high it was from my current vantage point, it had to be fifty feet tall or more. As I was drawn nearer to it, I began to hit the tree's roots as they grew farther outward from the central, bark-covered shaft. Thankfully, blessedly, the swirling mud began to slow as the oak appeared to reach its full height.

Great, maybe I can grab a root and squirm free before the dirt solidifies again.

Or not. I reached for a root, grabbing onto its rough bark-covered surface with slippery, mud-covered hands. Just as my fingers secured firm purchase on the thick, gnarled, rhizomatous growth, something latched onto my ankle beneath the surface of the mud.

"You have got to be fucking kidding," I snarled, just before I was yanked under and into the mud around me. I started to freak out a bit as I felt myself being pulled underground, deep within the root structure of the mighty oak.

Plant food. This is how I go out? Really?

I held my breath as long as I could, refusing to fill my lungs with the slimy muck that oozed into my ears and nostrils. I almost succumbed to the urge to inhale, but rough, muddy roots clamped around my mouth and nose, making it impossible to take a breath even if I'd wanted to do so. Finally, panic set in. I involuntarily began to shift into my Fomorian form just as I slipped into unconsciousness.

3

I woke to unfamiliar surroundings, vomiting up mud and expelling it forcefully from my nostrils. My hearing was muffled, as was my sense of smell, and my eyes were glued shut by what I assumed was caked-on mud and mucous. Cold water splashed all over my head, dousing me but washing away some of the muck clogging my ears.

"There's another pail just about a foot in front of you. Mind the tree's roots, though—else you'll crack your head and I'll have to heal you."

The voice was familiar—a man's voice, deep and sonorous. "Lugh, is that you?"

"One and the same. Now, clean yerself up. We've not much time before the old man's plan bears its twisted fruit."

I wiped mud from my eyes, which provided me with enough eyesight to locate the bucket. It looked to be made of a single piece of wood, but not carved or fashioned by human hands. Splashing water on my face, I cleaned away most of the dried mud—at least enough to enjoy the use of my senses again.

I wiped water from my eyes, pushing my hair back and squeezing the moisture from it in the same motion. Lugh was sitting on a large root a few feet away, smoking his pipe with a wry grin on his face. He looked much the same as the last time I'd seen him—like an actor from a light beer commercial.

He was a handsome deity, thin yet muscular, with curly blonde hair that fell in locks around his fair, almost boyish face. The Celtic god wore the same outfit as before, an embroidered blue tunic over loose tan pants tucked into supple leather boots. But this time he'd come armed, with a short sword in a tooled brass and leather scabbard that hung from a thick leather belt. A round hammered shield leaned against the tree's roots nearby.

He's expecting trouble. Damn, that can't be good.

"Lugh, if you're the one who pulled me from the ground..."

He scowled. "Pfah! Weren't me that did it, but the oak. Damned thing can't be made to harm its master, now can it? Not that I'd wish to see you come to harm or an early demise, not at all. But no, t'wasn't me who saved you from your own clumsiness."

"How was I supposed to know it'd do that? It's not like the Dagda put a warning label on the acorn he gave me."

Lugh puffed on his pipe and frowned. "All this time dealing with my kind and our progeny, and you still expect a gift of the Tuatha to be benign? If that's the case, you're not as sharp as I thought, not by half."

I nodded and coughed up more muddy mucous. "A fair point."

I looked around, taking in our environs for the first time. The oak tree was right there, not ten feet away. It was fully grown, with a trunk as wide as my mom's kitchen table and lush, leafy branches reaching to the sky. But the junkyard was gone. Instead of cars, weeds, and dirt, we were surrounded by a forest meadow straight out of legend.

I closed my eyes and took a deep breath, then looked at Lugh. "Um, can you tell me what happened to the junkyard? And please don't say it got sucked into the spell."

Lugh chuckled softly. "Oh, not to worry. The purpose of the acorn is not destruction, but creation. Yer great demesne of metal junk remains intact... mostly, at least, save for the space the oak needed to take for itself in your dimension."

"Dimension, you say?" I looked around again, realizing for the first time that I most definitely wasn't in Texas anymore. "Are we in Underhill, then?"

"No, we're in yer damned druid grove." Lugh tossed his hands in the air and sighed loudly. "Didna' the Dagda explain any of this to you?"

I tilted my head to one side, hitting my palm against my skull to get the water out of my ear. "Nope, not a thing. He just kind of tossed me the acorn and said, 'Here, you're going to need this. Don't lose it.' That was pretty much the extent of it."

Lugh rubbed his face. "Ach, but the bastard always was vague about such matters. It's not for me to school you in the ways of druidry, being as that's always been *his* thing. But since you fulfilled your end of our bargain admirably, I thought I'd take the opportunity to pop in and lend ye a hand."

"Speaking of which, how the heck did you get here?" I asked. "I thought the pathways to Underhill were all blocked off."

"Aye, they are. But the grove provides ways and means of getting just about anywhere, if you know how to use it. If I weren't on good terms with the Dagda, it'd expel me from here in short order. But for now, I'm able to use it as a doorway of sorts between the realms. At least, until he finds out that I came here."

"Something tells me your reason for being here has a lot to do with why the Dagda gifted the acorn to me in the first place," I muttered.

Lugh winked and puffed on his pipe. "That's fer sure. But don't think you can't use this place to your own benefit. It is *your* grove, after all."

I considered his words. "Since I planted it, that means I own it?"

He tapped his lips with the stem of his pipe, then pointed it at me. "'Own' is a rather tricky word, isn't it? It doesn't quite work that way. Think of the grove as a living thing, one that's more like a hound than, say, a hammer or a good pair of boots. You can be its master, certainly—yet you never truly own something that has a will of its own.

But treat it right, and it'll serve you faithfully for time and times to come."

"That—"

"Makes no sense, and every bit of sense in the world?" Lugh sat back against the tree's trunk, puffing thoughtfully on his pipe. "Yer dealing with the Tuatha now, lad. 'Tis no time to be dull. Yer dealing with powers beyond the reckoning of mortal men. Have some wits about you, or..." His voice trailed off, like the smoke wafting from the corners of his mouth.

"Or?" I asked, more out of spite than sense.

Lugh fixed me with a hard stare. "Or you'll be dead as a doornail, long before you reach your potential and serve your true purpose." He took an angry puff on his pipe. "That rascally Bag of yours is hanging on the other side of the tree, and there's a stream not far from here where you can make yourself presentable. I suggest you do so, and quick, so we can get down to the business at hand."

I waited for more, but it was clear Lugh had said all he was going to say for the moment. I decided to do the wise thing and play along, if only to see why he'd gone through the trouble of coming here. Truth be told, the last thing I needed was to piss off yet another Celtic deity.

4

I found my Craneskin Bag hanging where Lugh had indicated. I wasn't surprised, since it too had a mind of its own and always turned up eventually when we became separated. The stream was a short walk away—a picturesque brook running with cold, clear water, like an elven glade had been extracted from Tolkien's books and plopped down in front of me. I bathed quickly and changed, then headed back to the oak to see what was what.

Lugh stood with his hands on his hips, staring at the tree's trunk with narrowed eyes. "Ah, damn it. It's happening faster than I expected."

The tree looked pretty normal to me. "Care to fill me in?"

"You've eyes and magic of your own, do you not? Look!"

Taking the hint, I looked at the tree in the magical spectrum. The oak's leaves and branches shimmered and glowed with bright-green energy, signifying the life-giving nature magic that had created it. But something else resided at the core of the trunk—a roughly cocoon-shaped blob of druidic energy that glowed purple at the center, fading to red and dark blue around the edges.

"What is that thing?"

Lugh tsked. "That thing is the result of the pact the Dagda made with your former lover—or, rather, her spirit. The girl's ghost has taken up residence at the heart of the tree, and the grove's magic now merges with her spirit to create something new and potentially dangerous."

"Jesse? You mean Jesse is in there?"

Lugh crossed his arms as he nodded. "The same."

"But how? Why?"

Lugh rubbed his chin and gazed at the tree. "The Dagda means to resurrect her and, in so doing, bind you to his service through her. He likes you, lad, but make no mistake—he fears you as well. Fears what you'll become. Already those gods who remain amongst the various pantheons mutter about the 'god-killer druid' who slays their avatars and offspring. The Dagda would seek to control you, if he can, and make you his champion."

"So, yet another god wants to use me. No surprise there." I sat down heavily on a nearby root. "You say he's going to bring her back... why is that such a bad thing?"

Lugh gave me a sharp look. "I told you, have some wits about you. Resurrection is not a thing to be taken lightly, not at all! If he brings the girl back in this manner, she'll not be the same person. She'll be changed, perhaps beyond recognition—not necessarily in form, but in essence."

I rubbed my face briskly and ran my fingers through my hair. "Why are you bothering to tell me this? Why help me, Lugh?"

"No one said I was here to help *you*," he snapped. "Perhaps I'm here to help myself, eh?"

"I already figured that much. But what's your angle?"

"So, you're not as dense as you seem then. Hmph." His eyes and voice softened a bit, and he gave a wistful smile. "I'd be lying to you if I said I didn't have a stake in this. You're the first mortal in ages to show the Fomorian blood so strongly. That makes you a threat to the gods, and one hell of a dangerous pawn. For that reason, Niamh wanted to use you and the Dagda wants to control you—but me? Let's just say I want to see you set free."

"Free from what? C'mon, Lugh, stop speaking in riddles and tell me what you're really after." I glanced at the sword at his waist—almost certainly Fragarach—and the shield nearby. "From what I see, you came expecting a fight. What are you afraid of?"

Lugh crossed the distance between us in a heartbeat, grabbing me by my collar and lifting me off the ground. He pulled me close, so we were nearly nose to nose. Lightning flashed in his eyes as he spoke to me in a low, menacing voice, and I heard a roll of thunder in the distance.

"Watch it, little man. A budding demigod you may be, and cousin to me by blood—if a distant one at that. But don't think for a second that gives you leave to insult me.

I've many ways to achieve my ends, and yer but one of them."

I held his gaze for a moment, then nodded. "You're right. I shouldn't have challenged your honor. My apologies."

Lugh snorted softly before setting me down. "Apology accepted. Now, druid, I've a question to ask you. And before you answer it, think carefully and speak truly, for everything we do here today depends on it."

"I've no reason to deceive you, Lugh. Ask away."

"This woman—you loved her once, yes?"

I glanced at the oak and tried to swallow the lump that had suddenly appeared in my throat. "I did, and still do. Why do you ask?"

"And I take it you'd do anything to get her back?"

I hung my head, unable to look him in the eye—or even look at where Jesse's spirit now rested within the heartwood of the tree. "You know how she died, right?"

"I know, boy, that I do. You're not the first to be cursed with the Fomorian blood, after all."

"Then you also know I'd do anything to right that wrong."

Lugh's shoulders slumped. "Damn it, I was hoping you wouldn't say that."

"Now I'm confused. You were hoping I'd gotten over her?"

"Of course that's what I was hoping! Are ye daft, boy?"

I raised an eyebrow at the Celtic god. "I don't follow."

"Gah! You haven't been listening. The Dagda wants you safely under his thumb, and he intends to use the girl to do it. If he brings her back, she'll be changed by the grove's magic, which makes her a wild card in this whole scheme of his. What's more, you're a threat to the gods, which is why the Dagda wants you brought to heel in the first place. Surely his intentions favor the side of good, but do you really want to be his bloody brood matron?"

"I think you mean, 'his bitch.'"

"That's what I said!"

"Um, no." Lugh's nostrils flared slightly. "I mean, yeah, you did say that—in a manner of speaking. And no, I don't want to be anyone's 'brood matron.'"

Lugh threw his hands in the air. "Of course you don't. You'll understand why I wished you felt differently about the lass... being that I have to kill her now."

5

"Whoa, whoa, whoa—slow your roll there, Goldilocks. What do you mean you have to kill her?"

Lugh's eyes narrowed. "I'm going to let that one pass, just this once." He rested a hand lightly on his sword's pommel. "Now, as fer yer girlfriend, she's dead already—so I'd not be killing her so much as killing the thing growing within that tree that'll soon house her spirit. That way, the Dagda can't use her for leverage against you, to bring you into his service directly."

"But what if I want her to come back? Who says I even care she'll be changed?"

The Celtic deity's voice took on a somber tone. "I know it's hard, lad, but she'll be a liability to you in every way possible. Trust me when I say that she'll not be the woman you remember. Yet you'll love her all the same, even as the Dagda uses her to pull at your heartstrings like wires on a puppet's limbs. I have to put her down. There's no other way."

"I can't let you do that. I'd die to protect her."

"Think carefully now, lad, about what yer saying. She's already a ghost, and by rights she should've moved on to the next life. Sadly, this bond you two share has kept her from the eternal reward. If she takes physical form again, it'll only make it worse. She'll be immortal, and a demigod in her own right. What happens when you age and die, or fall in battle, and she's left to mourn your passing? Consider the consequences!"

I took a few steps, placing myself between Lugh and the oak. Then I reached into my Bag, drawing the flaming sword. I set it tip-down in front of me, resting my hands atop the pommel.

"I appreciate your intent, Lugh—really, I do. But you'll harm Jesse over my dead body."

Lugh shook his head and exhaled heavily. "Ach, I was afraid ye'd say that." He dropped his hand to the hilt of his sword, wrapping his fingers slowly around the grip. "Now, I promise I'll make this quick—"

Crack! Lugh's words were cut off as the oak split open with an earth-shattering sound, followed by a burst of magical energy that tossed me across the meadow, straight into the Celtic deity. My sword went flying as we landed in a tumble of arms and legs, each of us momentarily entangled until Lugh tossed me off him.

I landed several feet away, rolling groggily to my feet as I turned to see what had happened. Blindingly-bright green light suffused the area in and around the oak, obscuring whatever was going on there. Lugh stood, drawing his sword, the blade singing a low keening wail as it cleared the scabbard.

I looked around for my sword, spotting it nearby. Just as I was about to dive for it, I felt a length of cold, humming steel at my throat.

"Stay back, or I separate his head from his shoulders. Don't tempt me, lass! All it takes is a flick of my wrist, and the Answerer'll cleave his gourd clean off."

Since I was facing away from the tree, I couldn't actually see who he was speaking to. And I didn't dare turn my head for fear of slicing my neck open on the supernaturally-sharp blade. Lugh *was* a god, and I trusted he had full control over his weapon, but my druid senses also told me the damned thing would spill my blood if I so much as flinched.

Nothing like a sentient, bloodthirsty magical sword to ruin a druid's day.

I decided to wait for whoever Lugh had addressed to respond. A woman's voice answered, mellifluous and haunting, but familiar to me just the same.

"Ooh, I like this new body! I gotta tell you something, you Celtic gods sure do know how to put a girl back together."

"Jesse, is that you?" I asked, remaining as still as possible.

"Huh? Oh, hi, Colin. Yes, of course it's me. Sorry it took me so long to get here, but I was stuck in that silly cocoon. Funny, the gestation period was supposed to take weeks—but I guess the grove decided to speed things up when Bob Ross here made the mistake of threatening you."

Lugh shifted his weight slightly, although the sword didn't move one millimeter. "Listen here, lassie—one more step, and yer boyfriend becomes the next Dullahan. Even the grove won't be able to heal him from a mortal wound caused by this blade—you know it to be true."

Jessie yawned. "True. Then again, it's not like the grove would allow him to be injured, either."

"Do you care to place a wager on that?" the youthful god asked.

Jesse muttered to herself as if we weren't there. "Gah, I'm not sure how I feel about the patches of bark on my skin. Must be a side effect of speeding up the maturation process."

"I'll kill him, girl!" Lugh hissed.

"No, you won't," she replied listlessly, the boredom in her voice evident.

I heard someone snap their fingers, and suddenly I was on the other side of the oak, hand-in-hand with someone who stood just behind me to my left. I turned my head slowly, not wanting to get my hopes up, yet anticipating a moment I'd wished for since the day she'd died.

The first thing I noticed was her eyes. Instead of an iris, pupil, and sclera, each gleaming orb was colored a single shade of deep forest green. Despite their strangeness, those eyes were familiar—as were her fine, almost elfish features and the bright, broad smile she gave me.

"Hiya, Slugger."

She looked different but the same. I knew instantly

that the strange eldritch creature beside me was the same girl I'd loved from the moment we'd met. The way she stood, the angle at which she cocked her head as she smiled, how her pinkie finger twitched nervously as she waited for me to speak—everything told me this was the love of my life, come back from the grave.

"Jesse!" I exclaimed as I pulled her into a tight embrace.

6

"How? I mean, why? What—"

She pulled away, shushing me with a finger on my lips.

"Wish we had more time to catch up, but there's a god who wants to kill me on the other side of this grove. Right now, the grove and I are confusing him by reconfiguring the scenery, but eventually he's going to figure out a way to see past our magic. And unfortunately, I can't expel him from here."

"Why not?" I asked, still marveling at the fact that she was standing right in front of me. Well, not *her*, exactly— but close enough.

Jesse poked me in the chest with a slender, light-green finger. "Because you're the boss here, cupcake. Your house, your rules. That means *you* have to kick his ass out."

"Jess, this is Lugh Lámfada we're talking about here. That sword he's carrying is known as the Retaliator for a reason. It can cut through just about anything, and once it wounds a man, they never recover."

Jesse crinkled her nose and squinted at me. "Geez, Colin, when did you become such a pussy? He may be a god—emphasis on the small 'g,' mind you—but he's not invincible. C'mon, you have the home field advantage. Go out there and show him what's what, and I'll give you a hand when and where I can."

I furrowed my brow as she shoved me toward the other side of the tree. "Um, I don't think this is a very good idea..."

"Pish posh. Captain Jheri Curl doesn't stand a chance against you on your own turf. Now, go out there and kick his ass. While you're handling that prick, I'm going to make myself scarce so he doesn't plant that nasty sword in me. 'Kay? Great, see you in a few!"

She patted me on the cheek and disappeared, leaving a cloud of sun sparkles and green faery dust behind that quickly dissipated. A second later, all that was left was the light smell of lavender and freshly-turned earth.

Lugh's voice echoed from somewhere on the far side of the oak tree. "Druid, you may as well come out and face me. I'll not harm ye any more than necessary, and then I'll take care of that abomination that was once yer true love. Short, sweet, and painless is how I'll make her passing, I swear it."

"I can't let you do that, Lugh. Why don't we just talk this whole thing out?"

"There ye are," he replied in a low voice.

I heard a sort of whistling, sizzling whine that rapidly

grew in volume. I hit the deck, which was the first smart thing I'd done all day. A split-second after dropping to my hands and knees, a fiery missile burned a hole in the druid oak as it passed not six inches above my head. As my eyes tracked its path, the spear known as the Slaughterer flew into the distance only to make a broad, circular arc before retracing its path as it returned to the hand of its master.

Hadn't expected that—damned thing's supposed to be welded to the other Treasures and blocking the portals to Underhill back on Earth.

"What the fuck, Lugh? What happened to not harming me any more than necessary?"

Lugh laughed like a sociopath, reminding me that I was dealing with a god—and one of the progenitors of the fae to boot. "Come now, druid—don't be such a mammy's boy. What's the harm in a wee lobotomy between friends?"

I sank to my belly behind the oak tree as I hollered my reply. "Need I remind you that I'm not immortal? And that if you kill me, I won't come back to life in a century or two, resurrected and good as new?"

"Quit yer yammerin', druid. You and I both know the Fomorian blood won't allow you to die. 'Sides, I'm merely attempting to bring you *close* to death, not kill you. It's hardly the same thing."

"Small comfort, that," I muttered, marveling as I watched the smoking hole in the oak tree heal itself. If I took a hit like that in this form, I wasn't sure I could shift quickly enough to prevent my demise—even if I transformed involuntarily. I'd have to find a way to expel him

28

from the grove before I was forced to test the limits of my healing abilities.

One problem at a time. First, I'd best find the bastard before he finds me.

Muttering a cantrip to enhance my hearing, I held my breath and focused on determining Lugh's position in relation to my own. Just when I thought I'd located the Celtic god, Jesse popped her head out of the foliage above me, nearly making me jump out of my boots.

"My, but we're twitchy. Might be time to lay off the caffeine, champ."

"Damn it, Jesse—I nearly pissed my pants!"

She rolled her eyes. "I don't know why you're so worked up. It's not like he has the upper hand here. Besides, you know he can't do that thing you do, right?"

I pursed my lips and scowled. The new Jesse was turning out to be a major pain in the ass. "What thing? Could you be more specific, being as how one of the most powerful deities in the Celtic pantheon is gunning for us at this very moment?"

"Duh. What do you think I mean? That shifting thing. Personally, I don't care to see that side of you, because it still gives me nightmares. But it'd probably give you the edge you need to survive, at least until you figure out how to banish him."

"You might be right, but that side of me hasn't exactly been cooperating lately."

"A human can't fight a god, Colin. Not more than a few seconds, anyway." Jesse's head snapped to the right. "Uh-oh, looks like Shirley Temple is headed this way, so I gotta bounce. If I were you, I'd start shifting—like, now." She ducked back into the foliage, effectively disappearing from view.

"Thanks for all your help!" I whispered sotto voce at the expanse of leaves and branches above.

That outburst turned out to be a mistake. Seconds later, I heard that weird crackling whistle coming at me again. I ducked and rolled, but not quickly enough. Searing agony shot through me as the white-hot spearhead sliced my shoulder, cauterizing the wound immediately as it parted skin and muscle.

Ignoring the pain, I rolled six feet to my right, just to ensure the damned thing didn't skewer me on its return trip. After the spear passed overhead, I took off at a sprint into the woods, clutching my injured shoulder and wishing like hell I'd never planted that damned acorn.

7

Blinded by pain, I stumbled through the trees until I found another stream like the one I'd bathed in earlier. I dropped to my knees and splashed water on my wound in an attempt to alleviate the burning agony radiating from it. Blessedly, the cool waters of the bubbling brook had an immediate and beneficial effect. As the water washed over the wound, the pain subsided to a dull, throbbing ache, providing me the respite I needed for clear and undistracted thinking.

Since I'd returned from Underhill, I'd been getting violent urges I suspected were coming from my Hyde-side. I'd once thought I had it under control, but now it seemed my other side was bleeding through even when I was in my human form. These urges had been growing stronger, day by day, and I'd decided my *ríastrad* was becoming a greater risk every time I used it. I worried that eventually, my alternate personality would take over completely and I'd be unable to shift back to my natural state.

Of course, that left me with a conundrum. Shifting was a risk, but remaining in my human form and getting killed by Lugh wasn't exactly how I'd planned to spend the afternoon. So, how was I supposed to deal with him?

Jesse had been clear that she couldn't kick Lugh out on her own. But why? Hell if I knew. In truth, I was still confused, and I had a million questions about the whole damned thing. Like, when had the Dagda decided to bring her back? Did they have some kind of deal between them? And, if so, did that mean I could no longer trust her?

Also, it was obvious she'd become a supernatural creature somehow linked with the grove. What were her powers and limitations? Was she part of the grove or separate from it? As the "master" of the grove, did I have some authority over her? If so, it might come in handy... if she turned out to be as much of a monstrosity as Lugh had suggested.

Jesse had done some pretty amazing things already, and she'd intimated that she was somehow plugged into the magic of the grove. Lugh had suggested this place was in another dimension—perhaps it was a pocket dimension, like the one inside my Craneskin Bag. The god had also hinted at the grove having some sentience... did that mean I could communicate with it?

Can I control the grove's powers as well? Only one way to find out.

I splashed across the stream, wincing at the diminished yet still significant pain in my shoulder. I traveled less than a hundred feet before stumbling across a dense thicket, one with plenty of foliage and tightly-interwoven limbs to hide me from Lugh. I circled it until I located a small, tunnel-like opening near the ground. Entering it, I low-crawled on my stomach until I reached a tiny open space in the center of the small copse.

Once there, I sat cross-legged and slowed my breathing. Then, I reached out with my mind and senses to connect with the life around me, just as I'd done dozens of times before. Previously, linking up with my natural surroundings had been a gradual, gentle process, kind of like waking up from a long, pleasant nap.

But now, here in the grove, opening myself up to the life energy around me was like taking a plunge in an icy stream. It felt like stepping out of a sensory isolation tank, like I was experiencing the full breadth and depth of my senses for the very first time. One moment I was inside my body, the next I was plugged into a network of sight, sound, touch, smell, and taste that extended throughout the grove.

I felt the breeze on my skin, but also on every leaf, branch, flower petal, and blade of grass that grew here. I felt the dew as it collected on the plants, slowly tracing a path downward as the gravity in this place pulled it down to moisten the earth below. I felt small insects, worms, ants, and all manner of burrowing things as they dug their way through the soil, aerating the roots of the plants above while leaving droppings that fed those roots with vital nutrients to help them grow.

I was inside a rabbit's mind—not just touching its mind, but living inside it as I sensed everything it did. At the same time, I saw through a fawn's eyes, feeling the ungainly strength in its muscles and sinews as it pranced through a meadow playing with its sibling. Then I was up —high in the branches of the druid oak, hooting with an owl as it scanned the forest below in search for its next meal.

The oak.

How could I have missed it? It virtually sang with power, from the far reaches of its root system to the very tips of its tallest branches and highest leaves. It was alive like nothing else I'd ever connected to, exuding magic and power the way the sun gives off warmth and light. I realized, in an instant, that the oak was what gave the grove... everything. Here, the oak was the source of all life— creating it, feeding it, nurturing it, sustaining it, and renewing it in a never-ending cycle of birth, life, death, and rebirth.

Was this similar to the earth itself, a representative microcosm of the world I lived in? If so, the repercussions were staggering. I felt more alive than I ever had, more powerful than I ever had, more *connected* than I ever had. And I knew instinctively that the grove, while powerful in its own right, held nothing of the force and energy the earth and nature contained. I knew I could tap the power of the grove, and that here, I could wield deific powers.

I wondered, what would happen if someone learned to tap into the earth's energies in the same way? What powers might they wield? What forces would be at their command?

Thoughts and possibilities swirled inside my head, at

least until a booming voice brought me back to the present.

"Druid! Come on out now, and let's see this thing done. I can't get at yer wee lass until I know I've put you in yer place. So quit'cher hidin' and face me like a man—or a Fomorian, if ye feel so inclined."

Well, Lugh, you asked for it.

I opened my eyes and stood. With a thought, the wound in my shoulder healed as the thicket's brambles parted, and I marched out to face the Long-Striker himself.

8

L ugh's eyes narrowed as I walked out of the thicket. "So, lad, ye grew yerself a pair of balls—and great green ones, if my eyes don't deceive me. T'won't help ye none, 'cept fer delaying the inevitable."

I looked at the sword at his waist, the shield on his arm, and the spear in his hand, considering my options against those famous, magically-enhanced weapons.

"I'm curious—how'd you get your spear back?"

Lugh shrugged. "I didn't. Goibniu helped me craft this one. Not as good as the original—balance is off a bit. But it'll do in a pinch."

I kept my eyes on him, not even daring to blink for fear of that spear. My fingers gripped my flaming sword tightly, keeping the blade away from the nearby vegetation. The grove didn't care for having fire in its midst, but I knew I'd need a magic weapon if I was going to survive the coming fight. No way was I going to use my war club, since I was pretty sure Lugh would be immune to it—he'd had a hand in its construction.

"One last chance, Lugh. Leave now, and we can consider this one big misunderstanding."

He snorted. "Hah! And leave that thing that houses yer girlfriend's soul alive to wreak who knows what mischief for the Mighty One's sake? Pfah! If you think Aengus or that Welsh fool Gwydion had tricks up their sleeves, you've not seen a thing 'til you've witnessed the Dagda playing his games. Nay, I believe I'll see this through to its conclusion and hope you don't suffer too poorly for it."

Fine. I'd been gathering power for a spell during our brief chat and held it at the ready. "Before we begin, a quick question... have you ever danced with the devil in the pale moonlight?"

Lugh frowned. "Have I ever whah—?"

I released the spell, cutting loose with both barrels. Lightning shot from my left hand, as well as from the tip of the flaming sword, which I now had pointed at the Celtic deity. Considering the power I had to draw on here, I figured it was enough to fry a bull elephant. My plan was to shock the shit out of him, short-circuiting his nervous system so I could toss him out on his ass.

Unfortunately, I'd forgotten what Lugh was the god of —or, rather, what he primarily represented in the Celtic pantheon. Some would call him the god of light, but that would be a slight misnomer. His name was said to derive from an even earlier language than ancient Celtic, and had been translated by some language experts as "flashing light." Or, in modern parlance, *lightning.*

The Celtic deity pointed his spear at me, using it like a lightning rod to catch the spell I'd tossed at him. Instead of running down the shaft into his body, the energy gathered and danced around the flaming tip in an electric nimbus of ball lightning. It combined with the spear's magical fire until the spearhead crackled and hissed with heat and electricity, flashing alternately as it cycled back and forth between yellow-orange flames and white-hot sparks of magical power.

Lugh smiled like a snake about to strike. "My turn, lad."

Oh, shit.

The Celtic god pointed the spear at my head as he released a huge ball of electrical fire that shot forth like a rocket-propelled grenade. I acted without thought, gesturing with my hand as I muttered the words for *shield* and *stone* in Gaelic.

"Sciath cloiche!"

The words had no inherent power to speak of, but they served as a means of focusing my intent in magical form as I cast spells. Finnegas had taught me to use Gaelic for spellwork, to avoid accidentally triggering a spell during normal speech. Doing so was second nature now, and I silently thanked him for drilling me on my basic Gaelic over the last several weeks.

No sooner had I spoken the words than a huge monolithic shard of stone shot up from the ground, shielding me from Lugh's counterattack. I ducked just the same, covering my head and eyes with my arms as I huddled close to the stone, because I knew how much energy I'd put into that lightning spell. As expected, the top half of my stone barrier exploded into shards and chunks that peppered the area with rocky shrapnel. A small piece hit me, giving me a nasty gash across my ankle.

More lightning hit the rock above me, chipping away at my makeshift rampart bit by bit. All the while, Lugh taunted me as he advanced on my position.

"C'mon now, druid—izzat all you've got for me? That spell was impressive, and it might have worked on one of my brethren—but I'd expected much more of you than that."

Think, Colin, think!

I looked around me as I inched lower and lower to avoid getting shredded by granite shrapnel. Then, I looked at the ground, realizing that if I could make this huge boulder shoot out of the ground, I could also make something sink into it. I struggled to put together the proper words in my head.

"Duine a adhlacadh ina bheatha!"

I knew that I was close, but I couldn't seem to associate the words with the magic. Perhaps I wasn't quite ready to put together complex spells, or maybe I just hadn't internalized Gaelic enough to make it work. As I sought to connect the words with the spell I wanted, more lightning bolts hit the stone above me, hammering it down to a nub barely two feet tall.

I curled into a ball behind what was left of my hastily created fortification, wincing as shards of stone cut my arms, head, and back. Finally, out of frustration, I hammered a fist into the ground and spat out my intended spell in English.

"For fuck's sakes... bury him alive already!"

9

I felt a response that came from the very grove itself, one that was more of an impression than words. Couched within that impression was an image of the Celtic god being sucked into the earth and swallowed whole. At that moment I heard a sort of *plop!*, then the barrage of lightning stopped—followed by blessed, peaceful silence.

I waited no more than the span of three heartbeats, then peeked around the rock. *No Lugh. Huh.* But there was a bare patch of earth about six feet across, and my druid senses told me something powerful and pissed off was buried there.

Time to go.

I levered myself off the ground, using the stone barricade for support. Just as I got to my feet, Jesse appeared beside me in a swirl of wind and leaves.

"Good idea, burying him. But seriously, what were you thinking throwing lightning at him? He's basically the

Celtic version of Thor. That's like attacking an ifrit with fire. Not smart."

"Yeah, well—Lugh has a lot of skills and powers attributed to him. Sue me for forgetting about the most important one."

My ex-girlfriend-turned-dryad flashed me a lopsided grin as she punched me on the shoulder. "I guess no one's perfect—even the legendary 'Junkyard Druid.' Now, come on before he digs himself out."

No sooner had she spoken than the ground beneath our feet began to shake. "Um, I think maybe I didn't bury him deep enough."

Jesse shrugged with an annoyed roll of her eyes. "He was going to get out anyway, considering you can only bury him so deep here." She crossed her arms and tapped a finger on her chin. "Hmm. Colin, I'd say it's time to let Quasimodo come out and play."

"Are you sure that's a good idea? Because lately that side of me has been acting up—a lot."

"It's either that, or you get a reverse mohawk and involuntary trepanation courtesy of Lugh's flaming spear. Then, I get dead again—which pretty much ruins my plans for the evening." She waggled her eyebrows at me like Groucho Marx, fanning her hands down her body as she posed like a pin-up model. "Be a shame to let this all go to waste."

"I don't know how to respond to that, but I do know that I don't want you dead." I started shedding clothes, shooing her away. "Now, go hide—and pray that I can change back after going full-on Hyde side."

Jesse laughed as she strolled away, virtually disappearing into the trees nearby. "Oh, I doubt that'll be a problem—not with the druid grove on your side. And remember, you have the full magic of the grove at your disposal. Don't limit yourself to just what your physical form can do."

I considered her words as I stepped out of my jeans, stumbling a bit as the ground shook beneath me. I'd never cast magic in my Fomorian form before, mostly because it had never occurred to me to do so. In the past, I'd simply relied on that form's prodigious strength, speed, reflexes, and resilience. Well, that and the Eye's powers—but I had a funny feeling the Eye would balk at harming Lugh. I wondered what I might be capable of if I combined druid magic with my Fomorian physicality.

Probably be like combining the Hulk with Doctor Strange. This should be interesting.

Finally, I'd stripped down to my lycra boxer briefs. Jesse wolf-whistled from the woods in the distance. "Lookin' good, Champ!"

I sighed, choosing to ignore her for the moment. "Well, here goes nothing."

The change came much more quickly this time—almost instantaneously, in fact. Rather than a prolonged, painful rearrangement of my skeleton, skin, and muscles, I instead experienced a smooth transition from human to Fomorian. As usual, I gained more than a meter in height, and likely tripled my mass due to changes in bone density, skin thickness, muscle mass, and the like. But it had all happened within mere seconds, more like a transmogrification spell than a therianthropic transformation.

Even stranger than the ease at which I shifted was my mental state. I felt even more clearheaded than I had seconds before, with no inner battle between my human side and Fomorian personality going on at all. In fact, I felt *whole* for the first time since the initial onset of my *ríastrad*, as if I'd been put back together better than new.

After coming to grips with all that, I finally noticed a distinct absence. The Eye was silent. *No, not just silent —gone.*

It was as though it had never even been there. Whether that was due to its reticence to face its former master in combat or that it couldn't manifest here in the grove, I couldn't say. What I did know was that I was going to miss having all that power at my command. It'd served me well in battles with god-like entities before, and I was sure I'd miss its presence most keenly in the coming battle.

Well, then, time to see what tapping into the grove can do. I reached out again with my druid senses, but this time I was virtually flooded by the grove's magic. Before, it had opened my senses up to the entirety of the grove all at once. Now, the seemingly endless expanse of the grove's power hit me in a rush.

I looked down at the magical energies that danced around me, which appeared in shades of forest greens, earth-tone browns, and stony grays. Splashes of crystal clear energy spun in and out of those weaves; that was water magic, to be sure. There were rainbow prisms of light there as well, indicating the grove's ability to harness the light of the sun—or, what appeared to be the sun in this place. For all I knew, some distant star could be shining down from above.

I flexed my fingers and reveled in the power coursing through me. "So, this is what it means to be a god. Damn, it feels good to be a gangster," I muttered in disbelief. That's when Lugh flew straight up from the ground in a shower of soil and stone.

Guess it's time to do some gangster shit. Let's just hope I'm as powerful as I feel.

10

————

Lugh wasted no time in going on the attack, flinging his spear at me as he reached the apex of his leap from the earthen cage in which I'd placed him. I batted the spear aside, turning my body to dodge it as I extended my other palm toward him. With a thought, I cast a fireball from my hand that zoomed toward him like a rocket. It hit him in the chest and exploded on impact.

I knew it wouldn't do anything more to harm him than the lightning spell I'd cast earlier, but that wasn't the point. I merely wanted to distract him so I could close the distance and keep him from drawing that damned sword. No matter how much magic I commanded at the moment, or how powerful I might be in this form, I'd be finished with one swipe from that blade.

As expected, the Celtic deity shielded his eyes from the fireball's blast. In the time it took for the explosion's flash to dissipate, I was on him. I grabbed his wrists, placing both in my left hand as I snatched his sword and scabbard with my right. As I ripped his sword from his waist, I tossed it in a high arc over my shoulder.

"Jesse, see to it that our guest doesn't get that back 'til he leaves," I shouted.

"On it!" a voice called out from somewhere behind me.

Lugh glowered at me. "Oh, you'll pay fer that, you will," he hissed.

He jumped and kicked me in the chest with both feet, a move that was only possible because I was so much taller than him in my current state. Despite his human-sized stature, his booted feet hit me like battering rams, breaking my grip and sending me staggering away from him. The fair-haired god did a flip in the air, landing in a three-point stance a few meters away, his face split in an angry grin. He pushed off the ground, rising to his full height in one smooth motion.

"Yer strong, I'll give you that. But don't be thinkin' that just cause yer bigger, ye have an advantage. Remember, I cut my teeth by besting my kin—Fomorian and Tuatha alike. And you've a long way ta go before you can fill their boots, druid."

Awful talkative, all of a sudden. Gotta be stalling. Why is he—

I ducked to the side as the weird keening whistle of Lugh's spear flew past me, barely nicking my ear and burning the hair from that side of my head. The spear slapped into the god's hand, and he spun it around to tuck it under his arm like a quarterstaff.

"Damn it, Lugh—that could've taken my head off!"

"You'd just grow another one." He strutted toward me,

more swagger than Jagger, twirling his spear in dizzying patterns with apparent ease. "Now, then, let's get this thing over with. After I slay yer lass, I've got a date with this cute little Norse goddess, Sjöfn. Been working on her fer a few decades now, and damned if I'll miss out on yer account."

The spear had me worried, since I didn't currently have a weapon at hand. Besides, my sword was way too small for me in my Fomorian form, and my club wasn't an option. *If I only had something to match that spear...*

The thought had barely crossed my mind when a sapling sprouted from the ground directly in front of me. In an instant, the tree shot up to a certain height, perhaps half-again as tall as I was, shedding its leaves and bark to reveal dark, smooth wood underneath. It then morphed into the rough shape of a wooden spear, not unlike the whalebone *taiaha* my friend Hemi had once wielded.

No fool, I snagged it by the shaft, snapping the butt cleanly from its roots at the base. The weapon was perfectly sized, weighted, and balanced for me in my Fomorian form. *Weird. Ask, and ye shall receive...*

Apparently, Lugh wasn't as impressed by the grove's gift as I was. He spun his spear around and launched the tip at my face, quick as an adder's strike. Had I been in my human form, I would've eaten the fiery tip for sure. But in my Fomorian form my reflexes took over, and I found myself parrying Lugh's attack with my own weapon. Six more thrusts came in rapid succession, the god's attacks flowing like water as he danced and spun, dove low and high, and attacked much the same.

I blocked, parried, and dodged each attack, but his

speed was such that I was unable to launch a counterattack of my own. Just as the Dagda had worn me down when we'd sparred, Lugh was running me in circles as I backpedaled away from his attacks. And he did so with a seemingly endless supply of energy, never getting winded or showing a single sign of fatigue.

I knew from experience that, while I had much greater reserves of endurance in this form, I could still tire. Obviously, that concerned me a great deal. *What I need to do is tie him up so I can beat him down... but how?*

Again, no sooner had I thought it than the grove responded. Roots and vines shot out of the ground at Lugh's feet, seeking to wrap themselves around his ankles and feet.

He snickered. "I wondered when you'd be figuring that trick out." Lugh whipped the flaming spearhead around to slash himself free, while somehow managing to keep his attacks coming at the same time.

It was brilliant weapon-work, and I'd have said so if he hadn't been trying to take my head off. How he managed to maintain his advance, avoid being tripped up, slice through the vines and roots, and keep up his attacks on me, I had no idea. I realized that being a god wasn't just about power, but about all the skill one might acquire through centuries upon centuries of study and practice. That level of expertise, gained over his many millennia of existence, was something I'd never be able to match.

I'd have to trick him instead.

11

I began to backpedal in a specific direction, allowing the grove to direct my steps, intuitively aware as I got closer to my destination. *There.* I felt the presence of the druid oak behind me and altered the path of my retreat to skirt the trunk in a clockwise fashion. Just as instinct told me where the tree was in relation to my position, I also instinctively knew that circling the tree would take me back to the human realm.

But Lugh didn't know that.

"You'll not be able to hide behind that tree fer long, druid!" Lugh exclaimed. "And once I wear you down, it'll be just a quick stab to the noggin, then I'll kill the dryad and be off to meet that Nordic beauty. Oh, but she has an arse on her. Don't you fret now—the grove'll heal you, and eventually you'll get over the lass again as you did before."

"Fuck you, Lugh," I spat, grunting with exertion as I blocked a particularly hard swing of his spear. "It's not—your choice—to make!"

Just one more time around the oak...

"The hell if it isn't, lad. I'm a god, and I do as I please. Now, if you'd quit fighting, we could—"

The transition from the grove to the junkyard was jarring—or, at the very least, distracting. By the look on his face, I knew Lugh wasn't expecting it. He *was* a god, and probably never had to use the same methods of dimensional travel as a human. Heck, he probably just formed the thought in his mind and traveled wherever he wanted to go. And a single moment of surprise was all I needed.

I grabbed the shaft of his spear, at the same time spinning my own weapon around in a short arc to strike him in the temple. Lugh, being a deity and no mortal man, was merely stunned by the blow. However, it was enough to loosen his grip on his weapon. I kicked him in the chest, punting him across the junkyard. He landed against an old panel van, caving the side in on impact.

I knew the exact words to say, thanks to my connection to the grove. "I banish you, Lugh Lámfada, three times do I banish you. I banish you by the sun, moon, and stars, Lugh Lonnbéimnech, from my demesne. I banish you by the power of all druidry, Lugh mac Cein, from the home, hearth, and glade gifted to me by Dagda Eochaid Ollathair. You are banished, Lugh mac Ethlenn, begone and darken my doorway no more."

Unexpectedly, the wards around the junkyard flared with a greenish light as I completed the banishing. Tendrils of magic extended from all around the fence line, levitating Lugh high into the air. As the ward magic lifted him, the Celtic god began to stir, and he came back to his senses with a sad look on his face.

"Ach, but you've bested me, druid. And fer that, I commend you. But let it not be said that I didna warn you and did what I could to save you from yerself."

"Goodbye, Lugh," I said, waving his half-assed apology away with a flick of my hand. In response to my direction, the magic tendrils stretched like rubber bands, arcing up in the air overhead. Then, they flung Lugh off into the night.

"Remember, druid—I warned youuuuu...!" he hollered as his voice trailed off into the night.

I shook my head, wondering if I should have listened to him. Then I realized I still had his spear. *Better keep it safe—he's going to want it back.* I returned to the grove by circling the tree, widdershins this time. Jesse was, of course, waiting for me right when I appeared. I tossed the spear to her.

"Put this wherever you hid his sword. I'm sure he'll want it back, and the last thing I want to do is piss him off worse than he probably already is right now."

"Way ahead of you, my love."

I was about to shift back to my human form, but something made me reconsider. "Um, Jesse?"

"Yes?"

"Why exactly was Lugh so intent on killing you?"

She placed a finger on her lips, cocking her hips to the side as she held the spear out at arms-length. "Hmm... I dunno. Ooh, it looks like he nicked you a bit."

My eyes followed hers down to my abdomen. "I don't see anything—"

I looked up just in time to see a fiery spear tip headed straight at my left eye. Then, blackness.

I AWOKE IN A FOREST GLADE, with soft sunlight filtering through a leafy canopy above. Birds sang a sweet song from where they perched in the trees overhead, and butterflies flitted here and there all around. I blinked— once, twice, then Jesse's face appeared above me. But it wasn't her, not really. It was Jesse, but different.

"Hiya, Slugger."

"Jesse? Jess, is that you?"

"Yes, it's me."

I reached up to touch her face, trying to reconcile what my eyes were seeing with what I knew. She was definitely real—or, at least, corporeal. I tried to remember where I was, and how I got here.

"So, I'm not dead then?" I asked.

She shook her head. "Nope, but you nearly were. After you planted the Dagda's acorn, the tree sprouted from the ground like Jack's beanstalk. You fell and hit your head, then disappeared. I followed you here, and this happened." She gestured at her body. "So, whadya think?"

I rubbed my head. No lumps or bruises. My eye felt weird, though. I tried to remember what had happened, but drew a blank after planting the acorn.

"I don't get it, Jess. How could you come back from the dead?"

She smiled, her deep green eyes flashing with mischief. "Just lay your head in my lap and rest, and I'll tell you all about it..."

THE GOBLIN KING

In which Derp learns why stalking a yokai is not a good idea, and once more encounters the juggalo goblins.

12

Simon Martin was definitely not happy he'd gotten out of bed this morning. Not happy at all.

"Damn it, Kenny, you anus wipe—where the hell are you?"

Simon, who was more commonly known by the moniker of Derp, had agreed to meet his best friend Kenny in an alley in downtown Austin. It had recently been the scene of a murder—or, at least, that's what the boys suspected—and they'd hoped to find evidence of said murder to present to their friend, Colin McCool.

Colin was a bit of a mystery to the boys, which was partly the reason why they'd become so fascinated with him. He was supposed to be a druid—that is, a druid's apprentice. Simon and Kenny had yet to determine exactly what that entailed. For the most part, they knew it had to do with magic—not the YouTube video, pull a quarter from your ear variety, but "honest to goodness Harry Potter shit," as Kenny described it.

The year prior, Colin had rescued the boys from the clutches of the local goblin clan, who happened to worship some sort of evil clown god. This clown god apparently demanded a human sacrifice and, by happenstance or fate, Simon had been the first such victim they'd captured. It had been pure luck that Colin had been at the carnival that day, and that he'd seen goblins lurking about the grounds. If he hadn't, Simon would most certainly have been sacrificed to the goblin's insane clown god, and Kenny likely would have been killed trying to save him.

Thankfully, Colin *had* intervened, and in the most fantastic way possible—with magic. Thus, the boys' fates were sealed, because no nerd in their right mind would ignore the revelation that magic was real. The druid had sworn them to secrecy, and reluctantly hinted at the possibility that he might one day teach Simon and Kenny about magic... but only if they laid low and stayed out of trouble.

Colin wasn't referring to the normal sort of mischief, obviously, but trouble of the *supernatural* kind. He'd obviously forgotten what it was like to be a fourteen-year-old boy, because you don't reveal the coolest thing ever to a kid and expect them to leave it alone. Oh, the boys had done their best to steer clear of the World Beneath, as Colin referred to it—but a combination of fear and curiosity had won out in the end.

So, they'd begun to tamper with magic, telling themselves it was merely to learn how to protect themselves. First, they'd checked out books from the library—lame, and useless. Then, they'd hit online book retailers, spending much of Simon's piggy bank money as well as some drug money Kenny stole from a local meth dealer to purchase books that purported to teach real magic.

Of course, those had also been a dead end.

Finally, they'd found what they were looking for in the far corners of the Internet. Simon had been the first to discover it, a network of secret chat rooms, bulletin boards, and forums—old-school nerd stuff—where users discussed the World Beneath in relative anonymity. Simon and Kenny had created online personas, and soon found that the little firsthand knowledge they had already gained allotted them a small bit of celebrity among the other believers.

Eventually, they'd made contact with a hedge witch, and she'd shared a few minor cantrips with them—spells for creating wards against evil and the supernatural. The boys had tested them by entering a house that was supposedly haunted, where they'd set up a circle of protection. As it turned out, the "ghost" was a *clurichaun* who'd chased off the previous residents, scaring them so badly that the former owners had left their entire wine collection behind. Clurichauns were known alcoholics, so after hitting a score like that, the creature had taken to guarding his stash with great enthusiasm.

The little faery had tried to frighten off the boys in the usual manner to no avail. After that, he'd tried to curse them. Upon finding they were warded against simple magic, the clurichaun had attacked them physically in a blind rage. The alcoholic faery had made every attempt to dismember the boys with a rusty butcher knife, but thankfully it had been too drunk to be much of a threat. Eventually, the boys had convinced the clurichaun that they weren't there to steal his wine, and he'd allowed them to leave in peace.

Rather than being deterred by their close call with death, Simon and Kenny had been emboldened by the experience. Now, they were determined to prove to Colin that they were indeed worthy to learn the ways of magic. They intended to do so by exposing some previously unknown supernatural evil, which they then planned to bring to the druid's attention.

And that was why Simon was creeping around a dark alley in downtown Austin at night, alone, and wondering why the hell his best friend had bailed on him.

Clunk!

A loud noise came from deeper in the alley, like someone or something banging against a dumpster.

"Kenny! Is that you?"

Simon was no hero, but he also wanted very badly to impress Colin. In his estimation, the only way to do that was to prove that he and Kenny were just as sharp of mind and resourceful as the druid himself. Despite the fact that his hands were shaking and his knees felt weak, he pulled out his phone and activated a flashlight app, shining it into the far corners of the alley.

Oh, that's not good, the boy thought to himself as he saw what the light had revealed. In the darkest part of the alley, a large insectile creature squatted over a man's body. This thing was mostly humanoid in appearance, but it had way too many arms and legs and eyes, and teeth that marked it to be anything *but* human. That was, if the extra arms and legs and insect eyes hadn't given it away.

Simon remained frozen with fear for a heartbeat—then two, then three. In that span of time, the insect-thing's head snapped up and around, searching for the source of the light. The young man came to his senses then, shoving the phone under his shirt and jacket to hide the bright glare emanating from what his mother often referred to as his "electronic tumor." But it was too late. The thing had seen him.

The would-be druid apprentice's apprentice took a step back, preparing to run for his life. That's when something tackled him from the side, knocking him off his feet so he fell into the shadows. And kept falling, and falling, and falling...

13

Simon fell for what seemed like a long time, but then his prodigious backside made contact with a smooth, sloped surface. From that point on, he slid downward for a time in the darkness, but for how long he hadn't a clue. Thirty seconds? Two minutes? It was hard to keep track of time when your heart was pounding and you were pretty sure a man-eating were-spider was on your tail.

Eventually, the pitch of the slope leveled out just as a pinpoint of light began to shine ahead in the dark. Simon was smart enough to remain silent. He didn't know what had tackled him, or exactly how he had ended up sliding down this tunnel. Seconds later, he was gracelessly spat out into a large cavern—complete with stalactites above and stalagmites below, with water drip-drip-dripping all around.

He came to a slow, skidding stop against a particularly large stalagmite and stood to brush himself off as he got his bearings.

"Look out below, fat boy!" a high, whiny voice yelled, just as Simon's legs were taken out from under him. He tumbled backward, landing in a tangle with someone who smelled faintly of orange soda and rotten fish. This individual was dressed in baggy jeans, partially-laced tennis shoes, and a canvas Dickies hoodie with a stenciled, spray-painted depiction of a man with an axe on the back.

Simon was on top of the person, and could only see the back of his head. It was thick with ratty brown dreadlocks that stuck out in all directions from under a red baseball cap.

Wait a minute... that looks like—

A hand slapped the hard, damp floor of the cavern as the person underneath Simon braced to push themselves upright. Even in the low, flickering torchlight, he could make out clammy gray skin and long, narrow fingers ending in black, claw-like nails.

Goblin! Simon freaked out a bit and began battering at the person's back with closed fists. Not that his combative histrionics would do him much good, since he was much more of a talker than a fighter. But in the moment, he reacted on instinct instead of strategy or guile.

The figure in the hoodie responded by tossing Simon off him—not ungently, but not violently, either.

"Man, get off me, fool! Saved yo' ass, and dis is the thanks I get?"

Simon landed on his side, the ample padding of his torso saving him from any serious injury. He rolled to a sitting position, scrambling and crab-walking away from the goblin who had stood up to brush himself off. The goblin turned to look at him, his black and white clown makeup doing little to hide the sneer of disgust that split his face.

"Ease up, muggalo," the goblin chided. "I didn't rescue you for no good reason, homes."

"Ease up? Ease up? The last time I saw a goblin, you guys tried to sacrifice me!" Simon screamed. His heart pounded, and he thought he might be having a panic attack. "Don't tell me to ease up!"

The juggalo goblin raised his hands, spreading them wide as he backed away and sat on a broken-off stalagmite. "A-ight, I see your cause fo' concern. But you should know, if I hadn't Shanghai'd yo' ass, you'd be hanging from the witch's vampire tree 'bout now."

"Her what?" Simon asked, having calmed down a bit at the realization that yes, the goblin had saved him from the were-spider.

"Vampire tree. Seriously nasty shit. That spider witch be hangin' with some bird demon dude, and they both bad news. We been tryin' to stay away from those mothafuckas, layin' low 'til they get what they come for and split."

Simon nodded and looked around for a few moments, taking time to gather his senses. "How deep underground are we?"

"Shee-it, homie, at least a hun-ned feets. We goblins got mad skilz with digging tunnels and shit, even through rock and ore. Dwarves got nuthin' on us, homes." He noticed Simon looking nervously at the chute they'd exited from. "Entrance be hidden from pryin' eyes. We safe down here."

The young man took stock of his savior. He abruptly concluded that, at least for the moment, the goblin intended no harm. "So, why'd you save me?"

The goblin held up one long, crooked finger. "Now, that's a fucked-up story. Hang on a sec." He walked over to a beat-up plastic cooler, reaching inside and pulling out two bottles of Big Red. The goblin tossed one to Simon, who bobbled it before clutching it in his hands. "That's Texas Faygo, son. Drink up."

The goblin unscrewed the cap and took several big swallows, then wiped his mouth and belched like Will Ferrell in *Elf*. Not to be out-belched, not by anyone, Simon chugged half his drink and let a massive mouth fart rip.

His goblin companion cackled at the ceiling. "Damn, killa! I knew youse was a-ight. Now, whatchoo wanna know?"

"For starters, what's your name?"

The goblin pointed a thumb at his chest. "Skinny J. I'm the tribe's... how you wanna say... strategical playa? And I already know who you are, Heavy D. Every goblin in the tribe know about you and Special K."

"Special K? You mean Kenny?"

Skinny J nodded. "The same, homes."

"Why were you in that alley?" Derp asked.

"See, now you asking the right questions," Skinny J said, stabbing a finger at Derp and sloshing his Big Red all over the cave floor. "Here's what's up. We—meaning our goblin clan—been assed out since all that shit went down last year with the druid and the clown god. Since then, we can't get no love from our dark deity. Know why?"

Simon shrugged. "Uh-uh, why?"

"Because the clown god say our priest is shit, since he ain't the one who contacted the Harlequin from Hell. Nope. The Dark Jester says the only true priest is the one who sacrificed a life to him."

"That'd be one of you guys, right?"

Skinny J slammed the rest of his Big Red and tossed the empty bottle over his shoulder. "Nah, the clown god says we were just following orders. That's why I been like shade on your shadow, 'n why I wuz in that alley tonight. We need your help, Heavy D. The clown god say the druid be his high priest now, and without y'all's help, we 'bout ta go extinct and shit."

14

Simon "Derp" Martin had heard some funny shit in his fourteen years, and a lot of it had come from his own mouth. They didn't call him Derp for nothing, after all. But of all the crazy, hilarious crap he'd ever witnessed, nothing compared to the idiocy and irony of what Skinny J had just told him.

He tried not to laugh—really, he did. The goblins had tried to kill him once, and he wouldn't have put it past Skinny J to stick a knife in his gut and leave him bleeding out in the cave. Maybe it was nerves as well as the improbability of the whole thing, but Derp soon succumbed to an uncontrollable fit of the giggles. Meanwhile, Skinny J watched in silence, obviously feigning indifference to the young man's reaction.

"Oh, that's rich. I mean, really, that's classic." Derp wiped tears from his eyes, pulling himself upright after spending the last minute consumed by hysterical laughter. "You try to kill me and Kenny, Colin steps in and rescues us, and now you want our help? Wait until I tell Kenny about this."

Skinny J frowned. "Sure, go ahead 'n laugh at us. Everyone else does. Shit, it ain't our fault we the redheaded step kids of the World Beneath. Gods cursed us when they made us, man. Made us dumb and ugly so's no one would respect us. S'why we turned to the clown god, homes. Dat music spoke to us, and when we called out to the Dark Jester, he spoke back from the darkness."

Derp rubbed his face and shook himself like a dog in an effort to end his bout of hysteria. "Geez, sorry, man. I get laughed at all the time, so I know what it's like to be the butt of everyone's jokes."

Skinny J nodded enthusiastically. "It straight up sucks." He tapped a long, gray finger to his skull. "But I gots a plan, G. The clown god gave me something most goblins don't have—brains. I'm gonna lead my people up out of the ashes and into a new life."

"You sound like a motivational speaker, or one of those preachers on TV," Derp said.

"S'cuz I'm a true believer, homes. Juggalo for life, Dark Jester unto death. That's my motto." He paused and looked at the floor with a frown. "But the plan can't happen until we get right with our god."

Simon rubbed the side of his face. "Ugh, I can't believe I'm saying this... but how can I help?"

Skinny J practically leapt to his feet, pacing back and forth as he stabbed a finger in the air at Derp. "See? I knew you wuz down! I knew it! Now, all we gots to do is get that druid to stop beating us up every time he sees us and talk him into hustling us a human sacrifice. Think he'll do it?"

Derp spat Big Red all over the place. "Say what? Seriously? Uh-uh, ain't gonna happen. For one, that's guy's as goodie two-shoes as they come. Second, he's super preoccupied at the moment with doing druid just-your-shire crap."

"Yeah, we heard he went all Piggie Pie and shit. But we in dire straits, yo. Beggars and choosers, ya know?"

"I doubt Colin is your solution, no matter what your clown god said—no offense."

"None taken," Skinny J replied. "So, what we gonna do?"

"Give me a sec and let me think." Derp took a swig of the sugary red concoction and put on his thinking cap. If there was one thing he was good at, it was coming up with crazy schemes. "Jay, you said everyone in your tribe knows who me and Kenny are. Why is that?"

"Easy, homes. It's cuz you both was set aside as a worthy sacrifice to the clown god, but then you was spared. That means you special to the Dark Jester—holy-like. After we figured that shit out, we been watching yo' backs ever since."

Derp pondered that info for several long moments. "And what's all this stuff about extinction?"

"It's fer real, homes. The kobolds about ta wipe us off the face of the hood. We used ta check them motherfuckers good, put 'em in they place. But now word got out we ain't right with the Dark Jester, they think we weak. So, they be comin' at us hard, taking our warriors out one by one. If we don't stop 'em, we gonna be like that dojo bird."

"Dodo bird," Derp said absently.

"S'what I said, 'cept we don't do no karate."

Derp decided to let it slide. "Tell me about the kobolds."

"They's small-ass fuckers, all ugly wit' rat's faces and shit. Sneaky. Kobolds don't fight you head on like a stone-cold ninja would. Naw, they come from the shadows 'n shit, like little rat assassins." He nodded and crossed his arms. "Oh, and they into eighties rock."

"Come again?"

"Yeah, serious as shit. Kobolds are into eighties rock. Hair bands, man. Poison, Def Leppard, Mötley Crüe, Quiet Riot, Winger, Dokken—shit, all them lame-ass motha-fuckas. But the worst of it is, they absolutely crazy 'bout Van Halen."

Derp raised an eyebrow. "Classic Van Halen?"

Skinny J scowled. "Nah, not even. Hagar-era and shit. Might as well be lisnin' to Hootie and the Blowfish."

Derp nodded sagely. "That *is* bad. What's the clown god think of the kobolds?"

The goblin exhaled harshly. "Shee-it, he think they some bitch boy mothafuckas. And he think we gone soft, letting them bitches punk us. Me? I think it's why he done turned his back on us."

"Hmm..."

"Whatcha thinkin', playa?"

Derp smiled broadly. "I'm thinking I might have the solution to everyone's problems."

15

"A battle of the bands? Between goblins and kobolds? Are you out of your freaking mind?"

"Not just goblins and kobolds, Kenny. We'd invite the red caps, pixies, gnomes, trolls—heck, the more the merrier."

Derp's best friend sat back and took a sip of his iced mocha, extra whipped cream. He'd agreed to meet at a Starbucks off Parmer near the Samsung plant, not too far from where the boys lived. Kenny ran a hand through his hair, a habit he'd picked up not long after they'd met Colin. Derp knew his friend idolized the young druid's apprentice quite a bit more than he liked to admit.

"I still say you're crazy, dude. And besides, how is that going to help us convince Colin to teach us magic?" Kenny glanced around the coffee shop, lowering his voice as he leaned in. "I mean, he specifically told us to stay away from those kinds of—*people*."

Derp frowned. "Sheesh, man, why are you whispering?

Anyone hears, they'll just think we're talking about an MMO or something."

Kenny continued whispering as he replied. "It's not humans I'm worried about, Derp. What if one of *them* is around, and they hear us talking about this stuff? What if it's someone connected, or who's connected to someone connected, and that someone decides to silence us —for good?"

Derp laughed. "Since when are you into conspiracy theories, Kenny? Geez, I thought I was the nervous one."

Kenny scowled. "It could happen! Do I have to remind you that you almost got eaten by a were-spider a few nights ago?"

A middle-aged woman stood waiting for her drink nearby, dressed in business attire with a Samsung employee's badge strung from a lanyard around her neck. When Kenny said "were-spider," she turned and gave them a weird look.

"It's an online roleplaying game, ma'am." Derp held his hand up in the Vulcan salute and flashed her a silly grin. "Spock's honor."

The worker drone nodded and went back to checking her messages on her phone. Derp turned to his friend with a smug grin.

"See? These muggles are completely clueless. Heck, Colin does magic in public all the time and nobody bats an eye. People see what they want to see and believe what they want to believe."

"Oh, sweet Jesus, you're going to get us killed." Kenny

covered his face with his hands. "Just tell me what we're supposed to get out of this."

Kenny's rotund friend cracked his knuckles as he sat up, then he began counting items off on his fingers. "For one, the goblins know magic. They're magical creatures, after all. So, once we get them out of the dog house with their clown god, we can get their priests or shamans or whatever to teach us."

"I dunno, man. It sounds sketchy."

"I'm not finished," Derp continued, sounding a heck of a lot like Vizzini from *The Princess Bride*. "Second, we're going to prevent an all-out war between the goblins and kobolds that could boil over into the streets. Once Colin hears about how we handled all this, he'll be sure to take us on as his apprentices. So, if we can't learn magic from the goblins for some reason—"

"Like, because they won't teach us, or they sacrifice us to their clown god anyway..."

"—then we still have the magic thing covered."

Kenny arched an eyebrow. "And?"

"Finally—and this is the best part—we'll be rock stars in the World Beneath for putting this thing together! Celebrities! We'll have connections with all the major races once we're done. Among all those races, somebody somewhere has to know something about magic."

"But will they be willing to teach us without tricking us into giving up our souls, or casting a curse on us, or feeding us to their pet monster? I can't believe I'm saying this, but I think doing what Colin says is our best bet."

Derp sucked on his own caramel and caffeine concoction, slurping loudly through the straw as he ignored Kenny's misgivings. "Forget about all that. We need to talk about how we're going to make this thing happen. I'm telling you, this is the answer to all our problems. Every. Last. One!"

"Somehow, I doubt that." Kenny knuckled his forehead and looked down at the table before meeting his friend's eyes again. "But, you're my best friend, so I may as well hear the rest of your harebrained scheme."

"First off, we need to get Colin's help."

Kenny snorted coffee through his nose. He grabbed a wad of napkins and wiped his face, then the table. "Yeah, fat chance. Even if he would agree to something like this—which he wouldn't—I don't think he'd help. He's pretty pissed at me right now."

"Oh yeah? What'd you do?"

Kenny screwed his mouth to the side as he sucked air through his teeth. "I, uh, may have gotten him tasered. By a cop."

Derp's mouth formed an "O" shape. "Wow, dude—that's awesome!"

The boys high-fived each other across the table as Kenny flashed a Cheshire grin. "Yeah, it was. You should have seen him dance and twitch. Hysterical!"

"Tell me you have it on video." Kenny nodded. "Lemme see!"

"Later, man. If we keep talking about this crap, we'll never get anything done."

Derp sighed with genuine disappointment, then he nodded. "You're right. Anyway, I figured Colin would be a long shot, so I have a backup plan. We're going to need magic to pull this thing off, and I have just the person in mind."

"Oh yeah? Where?" Kenny's head swiveled around as he scanned the cafe for likely candidates.

"Not here. There." Derp pointed out the window, across the street and maybe a half-block down.

"At the trailer park? Seriously? Man, I live in a trailer park, and I can tell you there ain't no magicians living in projects on wheels."

Derp smiled and crossed his arms. "True, but this ain't no regular trailer park. You remember how Colin let it slip he was going to see some guy at 'Rocko's park'?"

"Yeah, I guess. So what?"

"So, dummy, Rocko is the leader of the Red Cap Syndicate!"

Kenny squinted at his friend. "Sounds suspiciously like a load of crap. How'd you find this out?"

"Meadow told me." Meadow was their hedge witch contact online. "She knows all kinds of stuff."

"How come she never tells me any of this shit?"

Derp rolled his eyes. "Because you're a dick, that's why. If you'd take the time to get to know people, instead of just getting what you want from them and bailing, maybe they'd tell you stuff."

"Ooh, look at Derp the player." Kenny pursed his lips in a sly grin. "So, you've been chatting with Meadow. *Derp's got a crush on Meadow, Derp's got a crush on Meadow*," he sang.

"Shit, dude, really? At least I don't look at porn all the time."

"It's research, Derp, purely research." He leaned back and scratched his head where his poliosis spot was. It was a nervous habit, and although Kenny liked to refer to it as a Mallen streak, it was just a white spot on the back of his head and not a streak at all. "Bet she's fat."

Derp shrugged. "So? You think some skinny chick is going to be able to handle all this? I don't think so," he said, imitating Rex Kwon Do as he finished the last sentence.

Kenny chuckled. "It's alright, man, I'm not here to judge. Meadow actually sounds kind of hot, when you think about it."

"Don't make fun of me and make it sound like you're not. You know I don't like it when you do that."

"I'm being serious!"

Derp sighed. "Let's just go find this magician."

16

The trailer park was quite a surprise. Located just off Dessau Road, a few blocks from an elementary school and not much farther from neighborhoods comprised of site-built homes, it was clean and well-maintained. The freshly-blacktopped roads were free of trash, the lawns neatly trimmed and green, and the mobile homes themselves in good repair. All in all, it was not what one might expect from a trailer park.

Kenny's head swiveled around as they walked down the main drag in the park, and he let out a low whistle. "Man, I want to move here. It's like these people actually *care* about their homes or something. Not like my neighborhood."

"Maybe your mom can meet a nice dwarf and move you guys over here," Derp teased. They were approaching the back side of the trailer park and had yet to see anyone who looked like a magician. In fact, they hadn't seen anyone at all thus far.

Kenny hunched his shoulders, glancing around nervously. "Sshh! Cool it, man—I think we're being watched."

Truth be told, Derp did get the distinct impression that someone or something was tracking their progress through the trailer park. Occasionally, he'd see movement out of the corner of his eye, but every time he turned to look nothing was there. Although they were traversing the neighborhood at lunchtime on a bright and sunny fall day, there was a certain chill and gloom in the air that gave him the creeps.

"Maybe we shouldn't be here, Kenny."

"Ya think? Well, it's too late for that, dipwad. Look." Kenny nodded ahead and behind them. About a dozen young teens had seemingly appeared from nowhere, blocking the road in both directions.

The youths were a motley bunch, male and female both—all wearing the sort of cheap, serviceable clothes that poor kids always seemed to wear with style. Plain white t-shirts and wife beaters, plaid Dickies short-sleeves buttoned at the collar only, blue work pants, faded and torn jeans, oversized football jerseys, bandanas, Converse All-Stars, and so on. They came in all sizes—some short and squat, others lean and wiry, and still others tall and willowy. One boy towered over the rest and was built like a truck. Derp thought he might be the leader, but he couldn't be sure.

Two things they all shared were their slightly alien features and the scowls on their faces.

"They don't look too friendly, Kenny."

"Just let me do the talking, and watch my back," his friend whispered.

"You lost?" a tall, model-thin girl with flaxen hair asked. She had the bluest eyes Derp had ever seen, and the fairest complexion as well. High cheek bones and a severe mouth confused the overall effect of her looks, and Derp couldn't decide if she was beautiful or merely interesting-looking.

Kenny shook his head. "Naw. Looking for someone."

The girl cocked her hip and crossed her arms. "Looking in the wrong place, then. This is a private neighborhood. Didn't you see the sign on the way in?"

Actually, Derp and Kenny *had* seen the sign. They'd also felt the "go away, look away" spell that had been cast on the front entrance, but they'd been able to resist the compulsion. The pair had recently taken to wearing their underwear inside-out, which served as an effective, if weak, protection against certain fae charms.

"Must'a missed it," Kenny replied. "Look, we just need to talk to this guy. We're not here to cause trouble or anything."

"Found it anyway," the big guy muttered, earning him a harsh look from the girl.

She stared at the boy a moment longer, waiting until he was sufficiently chastised before turning her cornflower blue eyes back on Kenny. "What's his name?"

Kenny looked at Derp. "Click," Derp said. "His name is Click."

She shook her head slowly. "Don't know anybody by that name. Leave while you still can, outsiders."

Derp noticed her doing something with her hands and realized a few of the kids were chanting under their breath. Suddenly, he found himself wanting *very* badly to leave the mobile home park. Very, very badly.

Kenny turned to his friend. "C'mon, man—we gotta leave, now."

Derp nodded as he spun on his heel to comply, his feet marching themselves toward the exit. Yet he was fully aware that it wasn't him who had decided to leave, but rather the suggestion planted within his mind by the girl and her friends. Even so, he was powerless to stop himself from walking away.

Do something, idiot!

Derp craned his neck around, making eye contact with the ringleader over his shoulder. "Wait! We're friends of Colin! We know Colin!"

Derp's feet continued their steady, relentless march toward the front gate of the park, but even as they did a small voice piped up from the back of the crowd of teens. "Colin McCool? The druid?"

The girl in charge looked over her shoulder with a frown. "Shush, Sal! We don't know these kids."

"But they're friends of Colin's, and if that's the case, that makes them alright."

A diminutive child stepped out from behind the crowd. He had ruddy cheeks and dark, curly locks that fell all around his face. The boy waved a hand at the rapidly fleeing pair. Immediately, it was like fog had been lifted from Derp's mind, and his feet and body were suddenly under his complete control again. Kenny was shaking his head like he'd been struck, but he appeared to be alright.

"I thought the underwear trick was supposed to prevent that from happening," Kenny whispered.

The little boy spoke up behind them. "There were too many of us casting the spell. If it had been just one of us, it might have worked. I'm Lil Sal," he said with a wave and cherubic smile.

Derp was the one to speak this time. "This is Kenny. I'm Simon—but everyone calls me Derp."

A few of the kids present snickered at that, but Little Sal simply nodded. "Pleased to meet you, Kenny and Derp. So, you boys know Colin? He's my very bestest friend, you know."

"I didn't know that, Sal," Derp replied. "But I'm glad to hear it. Colin saved us from some goblins last year, and since then we've kept in touch."

Sal's eyes got wide. "He did?" Sal covered the side of his mouth conspiratorially, whispering the rest of his response. "He saved me too, and a bunch of human kids— but I'm not supposed to talk about that."

By this point, Derp was absolutely charmed by Sal's forthright and innocent demeanor, as well as his almost infectious cuteness. He smiled as he slowly approached the child, earning harsh looks from the other fae teens. Ignoring their reactions, Derp knelt in front of Sal so he could get eye-level with the boy.

"Well then, I guess we got something in common— don't we, Sal?"

Sal nodded gravely, then grinned and grabbed Derp's hand. "C'mon, I can take you to Click. He's a friend, too."

17

Sal led them down the street a short distance to a small, dilapidated playground at the very end of the mobile home park. It looked like something out of the seventies, with a swing-set made from thick lengths of iron plumbing pipe, a merry-go-round that Derp was certain would sever limbs should one be caught under it, and a few of those wobbly animal thingies that always reminded him of the kiddie rides outside small-town grocery stores.

But what the playground didn't have was a magician.

"I don't see anyone," Derp said.

Sal looked up at Derp, still clinging to his hand. Derp thought that by now it would have gotten weird, but instead he just kind of felt warm inside. Safe. *Fae magic. What is this kid, anyway?*

"He's here. Or, at least, he was here. Or he will be here. Click always tends to show up on time, or close to it," Sal said.

"You needed something, little man?"

A lilting voice spoke from somewhere to Derp's right. Derp's eyes had just swept the playground a moment before, and he could have sworn no one had been there. He swung his head around, and there stood a youth who could have been fifteen, or seventeen, or twenty-three—it was hard to tell.

He had that ageless way about him that Derp had been told all higher fae possessed. The believers online talked about it endlessly, as it was one of the reasons people sought out the fae. Some people, especially those with chronic or terminal illnesses, thought the fae could heal them or grant them eternal life. Derp and Kenny knew this wasn't so, because they'd asked Colin about it. After finding out the truth, they'd agreed they wouldn't burst anyone's bubble—people needed hope, after all.

"And what have ye brought me now, Little Sallie? Two curious kittens, out to steal a sip o' cream from the milk-maid's bucket?" The youth's accent was weird and unfamiliar to Derp. He sounded sort of like one of those cartoon leprechauns, but the way he formed his words was altogether different as well. Derp also noticed that while he looked young, his eyes had something... ancient about them. This was no ordinary teenager, that was for sure.

"Not milk, silly—the boys are looking for magic," Sal said matter-of-factly. "Can you help them, Click?"

Click chuckled and ruffled the boy's hair. "I know what they're about, Sallie. Aye, that I do." Click looked at Kenny and Derp, taking them in with a sweep of his eyes. "Does the druid know yer here?"

Kenny tsked. "As if we needed his permission. We don't work for him."

Click chuckled wholeheartedly, as if that were the most amusing joke in the universe. "Ah, but ye do admire the cocky little twat, don'tcha now, boys? And if ye had yer way, ye'd be workin' fer him, just as sure as I'm standing here before ye."

Derp raised a hand in the air, waiting until Click nodded before he spoke. "You are standing before us, right?"

Click clapped his hands together, as if he were applauding a star pupil. "Belief—belief and an open mind! Such as these are the gifts of youth, my lad. If only the druid possessed those raw attributes, instead of that jaded brain of his—oh, what I could do with that lad then. Sadly, instead I'll have ta' teach him the hard way. A damnable shame." Click hung his head ruefully.

Kenny cleared his throat as he nudged Derp with his elbow. Derp glared at his friend, but he too was becoming anxious. All the teens were still standing around, glaring at the two boys and waiting to see if they'd need to intervene. It was unnerving, to say the least.

Click merely stared at the youths while affecting a pleasant look on his face. "Ye two boys had somethin' ta' ask me then?"

Derp froze a little, now that he was on the spot. "Um, Mr. Click—that is to say, Master Click, if that's what you prefer—"

Click interrupted him, nodding enthusiastically. "I like where this is going, lad—continue, continue."

"Well, the thing is, we're in need of a magician," Derp said.

"And ye were hopin' I'd be the one ta' help ye out."

Derp and Kenny both nodded at once.

"Fer what?" Click replied, his left eyebrow nearly touching his hairline. "There's plenty o' things a magician can be needed fer. Such as, thaumaturgy, necromancy, divination, cursing, healing, summoning, dispelling... why, the list goes on and on. Be specific, if ye want a yes or no answer."

Derp steeled his courage, deciding he'd better go for broke. "Well, Mr. Click—"

Click interrupted, raising his index finger in the air. "I liked the 'master' thing better—"

"Ahem, *Master* Click, what we need is a way to make music really, really loud."

Click frowned, thrusting his lower lip out as he tapped it with his finger. "I sense there's a wily and convoluted scheme at work here. Tell me more."

Kenny chimed in, answering in rapid-fire speech. "Well, there's these goblins—"

"And they worship this evil clown god," Derp added.

"Who is pissed at them, because Colin rescued us from them instead of letting them sacrifice us to the clown god—"

"And now they want our help to get back on the clown god's good side—"

"Because if they don't, they might get killed off by kobold ninja assassins—"

"So, we're gonna have a battle of the bands and invite

the kobolds, trolls, red caps, pixies, and anyone else who wants to compete, to play and see who rocks the house. But we need to make sure the goblins have the loudest music of all, because obviously we want them to win." Derp wheezed a bit as he got out that last part, so he pulled his inhaler from his pocket and took a puff.

Click had been listening intently to the boys the entire time, and he continued to tap his lip for several seconds before speaking. "Let me get this straight. Ye boys got abducted by goblins, who intended to sacrifice ye both to their evil clown god. The druid stepped in and saved ye, and instead o' wantin' ta' wipe these goblins from the face o' the earth, ye've decided ta' help them reconcile with their evil clown god so they kin survive a war with a rival kobold clan, and then wreak who knows what havoc on the local humans, and perhaps become a thorn in Queen Maeve's side as well. Izzat aboot right, lads?"

Kenny and Derp looked at each other. "Yup!" they agreed in unison.

Click's eyes narrowed, and he stared at them for several long, awkward seconds. Finally, he spread his arms in a magnanimous gesture as his face split in a huge grin. "Well, why didn't ya say so in the first place? O' course I'll help!"

18

The night of the contest, Derp was a nervous wreck. On the bus ride to the park where they were supposed to meet Skinny J, he threw up three times. Thankfully, his mom made him carry a barf bag in his backpack since he'd always had a weak stomach.

"Oh, why did I agree to do this?" he moaned, hanging his head in his hands.

Kenny smirked. "You didn't 'agree' to do anything. This was all your idea, remember?"

Derp dry-heaved a little before looking up at his best friend. "Don't remind me. Every time I think about it, my stomach flip-flops a little."

The other boy stood up halfway, taking a look around. "Too late to bail out now—we're here." He slapped his friend on the back with a smile. Kenny had at first been reluctant, but as they'd planned the event out he'd become almost enthusiastic about the entire debacle. "Look, there's Skinny J."

True to his word, the Juggalo goblin was standing just outside a streetlamp's pool of light, next to the bus stop in front of Walnut Creek Metro Park. He was dressed much as he had been when Derp had first met him, with the addition of several cheap-looking gold chains and bracelets—including a large medallion of a man with dreads running and holding an axe.

Kenny hopped off the bus first, but Derp paused at the top of the steps as another wave of nausea hit.

"You boys sure this is your stop?" the elderly bus driver asked in his Texas drawl. He was a wiry, older gentleman with long white hair pulled in a ponytail, and a mustache and beard that would have put Gandalf to shame. "Once you step off this bus, there's no getting back on. Last chance."

Derp thought that was an odd thing for a bus driver to say. He wanted to stay on the bus and call the whole thing off—really, he did. But he feared that bailing now would mean being hunted mercilessly by Skinny J and the rest of the goblin clan. He took a deep breath, balling up the top of his puke bag so it wouldn't splash and spill. Mom's spaghetti was a lot less tasty coming up than it was going down.

"Naw, mister, this is really our stop. I mean, this is where we have to go. That's, um, my uncle down there waiting for us."

Skinny J waved at the bus driver. Derp hoped his dark-gray skin and claws would look like gloves in the darkness. The bus driver looked at Skinny J and Kenny, then at Derp, and shrugged.

"Your call. See ya around, kid." He watched as Derp stepped off the bus, and to the boy it felt like walking the plank.

"What took you so long, man?" Kenny looked at his phone. "We're already late!"

Skinny J smiled at the boy. "Chill, young playa! I appreciate you is all eager and shit, but we gots all night to rain havoc on this mothafucka." The goblin turned to Derp, flashing wicked yellow teeth as his smile broadened. "Now, there be my little ninja—whaddup whaddup whaddup, killa?"

"Hey, Skinny J. Good to see you too." Derp tried to smile, but his stomach was still in knots. Then he realized he was still carrying his barf bag, so he tossed it in a nearby trash can. "Is everything ready?"

Skinny J nodded. "I pro-cured us all that shit you assed for, plus a tonna weed and drink. This gonna be lit, yo—muthafuckin' lit! Now, let's hustle on down to the venue and shit, so you homies can make it rain muthfuckin' chedda."

The goblin walked off into the woods nearby, which Derp noted were about as dark and foreboding as any he'd ever seen. Derp looked at his friend, and his friend looked back.

"You ready?" Kenny asked.

"Ready as I'll ever be. Let's just get this over with," Derp replied.

Kenny pulled out a pocket flashlight and lit the way into the forest. By the time they entered the woods, Skinny J was a vague, rapidly retreating shadow in the distance, so the boys hurried to catch up. Every so often, Derp could've sworn Jay's shadow grew, painting a much larger image of the goblin on the trees ahead. The goblin's shadow morphed occasionally as well, and if Derp hadn't known any better, he'd have said Skinny J's dreads looked an awful lot like a jester's cap in the dark.

The boy kept his wild imagination to himself, not wanting to insult the goblin or freak his friend out. Soon, Skinny J had led them to their destination—a large rocky outcropping, almost like a low cliff, that jutted up over a depression in the landscape. The goblin pressed on the rough limestone surface, and a section slid back with a low grinding noise. He turned and swept an arm at the entrance, standing aside so the boys could enter.

"Y'all first and shit, since you be the ringmasters tonight," he said with a wink. "But watch y'all's step yo, that first one be a doozy."

Kenny walked up to the entrance first, hanging on the side as he shone his flashlight into the dark. "It's like a funhouse chute—cool!" Kenny jumped in like a kid hitting the water slide at Schlitterbahn. "Wheeeeeee!"

His friend's shout of glee trailed off into the darkness below, just as Derp's stomach sank to his knees. He turned to look at the goblin. "Skinny J, what happens if the goblins lose?"

"Shee-it, killa! Ain't gonna be no loss for the goblin clan ta'night. Not wit' my lil' ninjas takin' care a' bidness." He slapped Derp on the shoulder, hard enough to sting. "Get on wit' yo' bad self—we 'bout ta' make history, Heavy D!"

Derp was about to apologize in advance in case he messed things up. But before he could speak the ground beneath his feet gave way, causing him to lose his footing. With a clumsy wave of his arms and a yelp, he tumbled into the tunnel below.

19

The chute spat the boys out in a smaller cavern than the one Derp had met Skinny J in a few nights prior. Tunnels branched off in all directions from the small antechamber, but it didn't take much guesswork to figure out which led to the concert. There was already a steady thump-thump-thumping of a bass line coming from the largest tunnel, and the electronic beat of house music pumping in the background. Every so often, they'd hear a crowd cheer in a chorus of human-sounding voices mixed with various roars, growls, and snarls.

Oh yeah, that's definitely the way to the stage, Derp thought.

"Where's Skinny J?" Kenny asked.

"I dunno—he was right behind me, I thought." Derp looked at the chute they'd just come out of and shrugged. "I guess we'd better get this show on the road, huh?"

Kenny pursed his lips. "No turning back now. Shit, dude. This is a lot scarier than I thought it'd be."

"Underwear inside out?" Derp asked.

Kenny nodded. "Three layers' worth."

Derp held up four fingers. "I had to wear my stretchy pants."

The boys broke out in nervous laughter, shouting "Nacho Libre!" in unison as they bumped fists. Derp sighed and headed down the tunnel.

Moments later, the boys emerged into a scene from a Salvator Rosa painting on crack. They were in a huge cavern, easily the length and width of a few football fields and half again as tall. It was lit up by flashing lights just like any night club scene or rave, except these lights floated around of their own accord, flaring and changing colors in time with the music. There was a huge stage set up to one side, along with a DJ booth where a tall, pale, willowy figure in white jeans, a white hoodie, white high tops, and dark sunglasses with white frames stood spinning records as she dropped a seriously sick beat. The entire backside of the stage was a wall of speakers two stories high, and the sound coming from them reverberated through Derp's body, rattling his bones and tickling his throat.

But that wasn't the craziest part. The craziest thing about the scene were the people and *things* on the dance floor.

There were creatures and figures of all shapes and sizes —small, big, skinny, tall, and everything in-between. There were little faeries who looked like Tinkerbell flying around, except they had really sharp teeth and were eating chunks of raw flesh from their bloody little hands. There were dwarves, goblins, little rat-faced creatures Derp was certain were kobolds, trolls, an ogre, and even a gargoyle perched on a ledge high overhead, watching the entire proceedings. Derp saw a few humans in the crowd as well. At least, he thought they were humans until one hissed at him, flashing long white incisors that glowed in the magic neon blacklight.

Before they had time to go into a full-on freak-out, someone grabbed them by the arms and started hustling them to the stage. "Now, now, me lads, it wouldn't do for ye ta' get eaten by a vampire before the night has even gotten started. The last thing we need is fer Luther ta' hafta kill one o' his coven just because you two tempted the poor bloodsucker beyond all hope o' self-control."

Derp looked over at the person who'd latched onto his arm. "Click! Man, am I glad to see you."

"I kin imagine, as you two boys looked like a pair o' deer in headlights. But, no time fer gawkin'! Ye have a show ta' run, and it's time ta' be getting it started." The youthful magician walked them to a set of steps that led up to the stage. He released their arms, then gently nudged them toward the stairs. "Go on, now—the microphone's right there at center stage. Introduce yerselves, then announce that the show's aboot ta' begin. The acts'll take it from there. Go on, laddies! Fame, fortune, and a one hell of a fracas await!"

Derp swallowed a rising tide of bile, then took that first intimidating step. After that, it was as if something else took over, like his feet were on autopilot. Before he knew it, he was standing in front of the mic with Kenny beside him.

The music came to a grinding halt, then all eyes in the room were upon them.

"Is this thing on?" Kenny tapped the mic, causing it to squelch. Derp gave him a look that could curdle milk. "Geez, I was just checking! It's your show, dude. Have at it," he said as he pulled the microphone from the stand and handed it to his friend.

The microphone felt like it weighed a hundred pounds in his hand, but somehow Derp managed to bring it to his lips. "Um... hi. I'm Derp, and this is my best friend Kenny."

Someone in back shouted, "In da house—whoop, whoop!" emboldening Derp a bit. He was pretty sure it was Skinny J.

"Anyway, we put this thing together for you guys—and goblins, and fae, and dwarves, pixies, sprites, spriggans, trolls, witches, vampires, 'thropes, ogres, brownies, red caps, clurichauns, leprechauns, cu sith, cat sith, fuaths, glaistigs, gnomes, gremlins, hags, harpies, kelpies, kobolds, merrows, púcas, selkies, sluagh, sprites, and yōkai, as I hear we have a few visiting from overseas. Did I forget anyone?"

A grumbling roar echoed from the ledge high above the crowd, and Kenny pointed out above the audience.

"Oh yes, and gargoyles!" Derp shouted. "Sorry for that!"

The gargoyle chuffed, then took a pose and went completely still.

"Anyway, we want to thank you for coming tonight. We also want to thank our hosts, the Axe Murder Juggalo Posse, who you all know as the goblin clan."

A few boos came up from the crowd, but those present mostly remained respectful. Mostly.

"Well, I could stand up here and jabber all night, especially after all the Red Bulls I had earlier, but I know you all came for the Battle of the Bands. Is that right?" Derp raised his hand to his ear, and the crowd cheered a little. "What? I can't hear you? C'mon, everybody—raise the roof!"

He thrust the mic out toward the crowd, and this time they erupted in the wildest ruckus Derp had ever heard.

"That's more like it! On with the show!"

Kenny and Derp exited stage left, heading for the sound box because that's where Click was standing. They flanked the magician, smiling like Pippin and Merry having a pint at the Green Dragon Inn.

Click clapped a hand on each of their shoulders. "Well done, lads—well done!" The magician rubbed his palms together, hunching his shoulders like an evil mastermind preparing to take over the world. "Now, let's see what this evening has in store for us, shall we?"

20

The rest of the night went by in a blur. In later days, the boys would be able to recall an overall impression of the proceedings, but much of it would remain hidden within a foggy haze that defied clear recollection. However, Derp did remember each act that hit the stage, and how they performed against one another.

The trolls came first, doing a weird sort of spoken word thing in trollish. Huge bass drums backed the two speakers, with an accompaniment of a few dozen troll warriors chanting and stomping—all of it done sans amplifiers or microphones. At first, Derp thought they'd get booed off the stage, but the whole act was as hypnotizing as it was logistically impressive. When they finished their act, the house erupted in shouts and applause.

The pixies did a cover of "Linger" by the Cranberries. It was haunting, but unoriginal. They were met by lukewarm applause as they departed the stage. The gnomes took the mic next, dressed in black t-shirts and ripped up jeans.

They did a long song in the style of German death metal, bobbing their heads and swirling their beards to the beat the entire time. When they were done, there was a ton of whistling and shouting. Apparently, they had a following among the crowd.

Next up were the red caps, all dressed in white shirts, black dinner jackets, and red fedoras. They came with a full brass band, along with a pianist and human female backup singers who Derp suspected were strippers. The red caps did a Frank Sinatra mash-up, and they did it surprisingly well, ending with the last few bars of "My Way." Rocko sang lead, and Sal's dad rocked a trombone on stage. They ended their set to strong, respectful applause.

Next came the kobolds, who came on stage with teased hair wigs, shirts that had been razored up until they were almost falling apart, and leather pants that were so tight they must've been stitched on. The little rat-faced creatures began with a scorching version of Van Halen's "Eruption," then they broke into "Poundcake," "Right Now," and finished their set with "Dreams." They were good, but they didn't bring the house down.

Finally, it was time for the goblins to finish up the contest. Derp had been sure Skinny J would perform, but he was nowhere to be seen. Instead, two goblins took center stage, both dressed in full Juggalo regalia— including white and black clown make-up that matched what their musical idols typically wore. The pair got booed and catcalled at first, causing Derp to look over at Click to ensure the magician was on the case. Click winked at the boy as he silently counted down... *three... two... one.*

Then, the beat dropped.

It had been apparent that the other acts had used magic to enhance their sound, volume, and delivery. That was to be expected, considering that every band's members were comprised of supernatural creatures. However, none of the previous acts could hold a candle to the mystical energies that currently shored up the pair of goblin rappers on stage.

Each thump of the bass line was like a lion roaring deep inside Derp's chest. Every line they uttered, every hook they dropped, every loop, every bar and break—all of it worked together to weave a spell made up of rhymes and beats and ancient magic.

In short, the Axe Murder Juggalo Posse brought the house down.

Derp couldn't remember much after that, but he did remember he and Kenny being carried around the cavern on the shoulders of a crowd of painted up goblins. He also vaguely recalled a bout of crowd surfing, and for once feeling like he wasn't the only person in the room who didn't fit in.

The next morning, Derp woke up in his bed, wondering if it had all been a dream. Then, he felt something around his neck, a chain or necklace of some sort. He pulled it off and looked at it—a small, gold effigy hanging from a thick gold rope chain. It featured the likeness of a dreadlocked man, running with a hatchet in his hand.

The boy laid his head back down on his pillow and stared at the necklace as it slowly swung round and round beneath his hand.

KENNY AND DERP never saw Skinny J again. However, they were invited back to the goblin caves as honored guests. Sure enough, the tribe's shamans were more than happy to share a few simple magic spells with the boys, much to their delight. The two agreed they'd keep what they learned to themselves, rather than risk the wrath of their goodie two-shoes druid friend.

A few days later, Colin showed up at Derp's house. He'd been looking for Derp all week under the pretense that the were-spider had taken him, and was royally pissed to learn that Kenny had known of Derp's whereabouts nearly the entire time. After a sound scolding, the boys were even more reluctant to fill Colin in on all the details of their adventure. They settled for telling him that the goblins had made them priests of a sort, and that they had participated in a small amount of chanting and rituals at the goblins' behest.

The druid didn't think that was a good idea—*at all*. The request had seemed pretty harmless to the boys, so Derp and Kenny didn't pay much attention to the additional chastisement. They'd proven their worth—if not to Colin, at least to themselves. And they'd learned some magic as well. In their shared opinion, they'd earned a major victory. That was all that mattered.

Yet something tugged at the back of Derp's mind every time he thought about his interactions with Skinny J. None of the goblin clan members seemed to know who the strange goblin was, nor would they acknowledge he'd even existed. Derp chalked it up to the fact that the goblins had difficulties understanding human language. In the end, he decided that some things were better left unexplained.

But every so often, he'd wake up and see a shadow on his bedroom wall—the vague outline of a person in a three-pointed jester's cap. One blink of his eyes and it'd be gone, but the boy knew—Skinny J was still there, "a shade on his shadow."

Did that frighten him?

Not this ninja, Derp thought to himself.

Juggalo for life, Dark Jester unto death, a voice inside his head replied. *Stay fresh, lil killa.*

GOING UNDER

In which Hemi dies and is transported to the Maori underworld.

21

So what's it like, dying?

Kind of hard to explain, really. One moment you're in your body, and the next you're not. To tell the truth, it's not the dying that's the hard part... it's the stuff that comes before that really sucks.

Take, for example, falling off a great big cliff. First, you take a tumble, and then you fall for a little while, then maybe you bounce off a ledge or a rock. A few things break, the shock of it all overwhelms you, and then you're falling again. Then you bounce off another ledge. A few more things break—let's say your ribs—and now you're finding it hard to breathe.

About this time, you start to think, *Well, maybe if I could catch on to one of these cliffs I'm bouncing off of, I might end all this torture.* Because by now, on top of the broken ribs, you probably have a leg or an arm that's been snapped in several places, flopping around with a mind of its own. Bones are grinding together, mashing tissue and crushing nerves, and you've really no way to stop it.

Logically, stopping your descent seems like a really good idea about now. That's why you reach out with an arm to try to grab something on the way down. And that's also how you lose most of the fingers on your left hand.

This is about the time you've hit terminal velocity. It's also roughly the time when you realize you're about to die. At this point, you start praying—not that you will be saved, mind you, but that you won't bounce off anything else on your way down.

Really, what you're praying for is a quick death. So, when you see the ground coming up at you, you don't shut your eyes. You just keep staring at it as it rushes up to meet you. And all that's going through your mind is, *Oh, thank goodness... blessed relief is on its way.*

That's when you remember your wards are still activated. Which is probably gonna mean the fall won't kill you—immediately, that is.

And this is why it sucks to be a demigod.

MY NAME'S HEMI WAARA. I know it's not the most Maori name, but it's the one I was given so don't hold it against me. Since I was little, I've always been a bit of an oddball. And, to some of my relatives, a real pain in the side.

My stepdad was the bloke who gave me the most grief. Can't say I blame him. No man wants to be reminded that his wife cheated on him every day of his life. And if you think mortals are jealous, you haven't seen jealousy until you've hung around with a few gods. Trust me, they take anger and jealousy to a whole new level.

Since I was a living breathing reminder to my good old stepdad that Mum had stepped out on him, well—you can imagine I wasn't exactly his favorite son. Of course, the first time Mum caught him trying to kill me, she took me straight to my real dad and told him to hide me somewhere that even the Maori gods couldn't find me.

Which is why I grew up on Oahu. But that's another story. Finnegas asked me to write all this down, and what I'm supposed to be talking about is how I traveled to the underworld and back again. So, I guess I better tell you what happened after I died in Underhill.

As my friend Colin would say, here goes nothing.

YOU MIGHT BE WONDERING how a Maori demigod ended up in the land of the Celtic fae. It's not much of a mystery, really, since my best friend is a druid and all tied up with the Celtic Pantheon. He doesn't fully understand just how connected he is to all those Celtic deities, but I do.

Not too quick on the uptake, that Colin. Good guy though.

Anyway, the fae had been stealing kids for purposes I don't care to talk about. The whole thing got my blood boiling, so when Colin decided to put together a crew to get the kids back, he didn't need to ask me twice. I followed him to Underhill, and that's where I died.

Kind of a shitty deal, that one. Turns out when you die in the realm of another culture's gods, it's harder for your spirit to find its way home. And that made it easy for Whiro to throw a wrench in the gears.

Since you may not have heard of Whiro, I'll fill you in. Among Maori deities, he's the absolute personification of evil. All disease and illness comes from him, along with spells that cause sickness and pestilence. Nasty piece of work, that one.

What's worse is he's always trying to break free of the underworld. But he's not strong enough yet, so he eats the dead to increase his strength. And, wouldn't you know it, eating the corpse of a demigod gives him a whole lot more power than eating human corpses.

When Whiro heard I died, right away he started scheming to eat me. He knew my mother could easily heal my body and return my spirit to it, and then raise me from the dead. She is the goddess who rules the underworld, after all.

Whiro couldn't allow that, so he used his evil magic to make sure my spirit didn't find its way back to my mother's house in the underworld. Instead, I ended up in probably the worst place I could've landed. After my spirit got whisked away by Whiro's magic, I found myself standing right in front of the House of Endless Night.

22

Now, there's something you ought to understand about the gods. You might think they're all ancient and stuffy—a bunch of twenty-foot-tall people with booming voices and somber looks, sitting on thrones, brooding on eternity by torchlight. If you think that way, you'd be wrong.

Contrary to popular belief, the gods have adapted with the times. You wouldn't know it, but many of them now live in the human world, interacting with mortals on a daily basis and living somewhat normal lives. In fact, you may have run into one a time or two and not even known it.

What's more, the gods shape their realms to suit them-selves. Take Miru's house, for example. You might think a place called Tatau-o-te-Pō, The House of Endless Night, would be a dark, gloomy, dreary cavern somewhere, filled with things you'd rather not see in the light.

Once again, you'd be wrong... at least on one of those counts. Miru's place was anything but dark and gloomy. Oh, there were corners of the place that you didn't want to be caught dead in—no pun intended—and there were definitely things that lived there you'd rather not run into, no matter if it was day or night. But Miru had adapted to the times.

Instead of a dank cave or dark and dusty royal hall, The House of Endless Night was a rowdy, loud, neon-lit pub. And it didn't look like some K Road nightclub, with electronic dance music pumping out of the speakers and lights flashing under a translucent floor. No, this place was more like some biker bar roadhouse you'd find on the sketchy side of Auckland—complete with tobacco smoke, the smell of stale beer and sex, and the distinct stench of dark sorcery and pure hate.

I'd been there once or twice, and the last time I was told in no uncertain terms that I shouldn't come back. I may have torn the place up a bit in the middle of a drunken brawl. Not like that was something that wasn't common in Miru's place. It's just that the normal patrons there weren't as destructive as I could be after a few dozen drinks. Miru didn't appreciate me tearing up his house— or her house, depending on Miru's mood—so he kicked me out. Permanently.

So, when I walked up to the front door and a giant blocked my way, it wasn't really a surprise. The bouncer had shrunk himself a bit to fit under the roof over the front entrance. He was still a few feet taller than me, about the size of that giant that had pulled me off the cliff back in Underhill.

"Hey, Matt," I said with a nod.

"Hey, Hemi," Matau said. "Heard what happened. Sorry about that. Must've been tough."

I sucked air through my teeth and cocked my head. "Things happen, you know? But I appreciate your concern."

"Yeah, sucks though." Matt stared off into the night, then fixed me with a stare that held just a hint of regret. He clasped his hands in front of him—two huge meat hooks I'd personally seen him use to rip someone limb from limb. The giant flicked a finger at me, a barely perceptible gesture. "You know I can't let you in here. Especially not like that. You've got no status. Some of them inside might decide to take you down. Help Whiro out."

I scratched the back of my head. "Think Miru would allow that?" Matt shrugged, his eyes scanning the dark behind me. "I still have to get in there, Matt. Got to talk to Miru before I pass through."

Matt shook his head. "Nope. Gonna have to go through me. Boss was clear."

I'd been expecting as much, so I didn't hesitate once the niceties were over. Matt's kneecap was right there, being the size he was. I kicked it sideways just as he was reaching to grab me and throw a punch. I parried his arms, twisting his upper body slightly as I pivoted to the outside. That lined his jaw up for a big overhand right that dropped him to his knees.

I snaked my left hand around his arm to get an under

hook on his right shoulder, then hooked my right hand behind his neck. This allowed me to control his head as I pulled him into my knee. I smashed my knee into his nose, once, twice, and a third time. He was dead weight by this point, out cold. I leaned him up against the side of the bar next to the door, then I went inside.

The interior was everything you'd expect from a roadhouse dive bar. Lots of exposed wood, plenty of neon signs, smoke-filled air, and the smell of stale puke, piss, and beer under it all. The bar's patrons all looked like rough types— a rogues' gallery for sure. They looked human, more or less, and in fact some of them had been human spirits once... until Miru's sorcery twisted them into something different.

I tapped the waitress on the arm to get her attention as she walked by. She turned to look at me—a pretty, dark-skinned thing in a skintight black T-shirt and denim skirt. For a moment, her glamour blurred and another face transposed itself on top of hers—something dark and reptilian, with long sharp teeth and a forked tongue that tasted the air with a hiss.

I pretended I didn't see it. Everybody here was more than they appeared. "Miru around?"

She looked me up and down, frowning in a way that made the facial tattoos on her chin look like fangs. "He's in back, but you probably don't want to disturb him. He's entertaining guests right now, so I don't think he'll appreciate an interruption. Especially from the likes of you."

I glanced around the place, noticing that more than a few customers were looking my way. "He'd probably prefer that to me sticking around out here and tearing up his place again."

The waitress popped her gum and shrugged. "Your funeral."

I chuckled and headed to the offices in back.

23

I shouldered my way through the crowd until I reached a dark and worn wooden door with a sign that said "PRIVATE" tacked at eye level. I paused for a second before I grabbed the chipped, enameled metal door knob and shoved the door open. It opened to a hallway that faded into darkness just a few feet beyond.

As I passed through the doorway, a chill went right through me. Dark sorcery, for sure. The Kiri Tuhi on my shoulders and back lit up slightly, Mum's *kaiwhatu* in the ink doing its work to protect me from the death magic spell Miru had placed here. Rūaumoko might have stolen my moko, and with it a great deal of my power, but he couldn't touch my mother's magic.

Even he wasn't stupid enough to mess with that.

I walked forward into the gloom, knowing it was just an illusion—darkness spun of magic and nothing more. After a few steps, the shadows receded and Miru's VIP lounge appeared before me.

The floor was dark wood, scuffed and stained with whiskey and blood. The only light in the room came from a lamp over the pool table, which sat in the center of the space. There were four people here, although you couldn't really call them that. One of them was Miru, but I didn't recognize any of the others. They were probably lesser gods of evil, since that was the only company Miru kept.

Miru was dressed like a real high-roller as usual—in glossy snakeskin boots, dark jeans, a white dress shirt, and a black dinner jacket. He wore a Rolex watch on his wrist, and each of his fingers were adorned with rings in precious metals and stones that glistened and sparkled despite the weak light. With his mocha skin, fine features, and midnight hair slicked back against his scalp, he might have seemed out of place in a dive like this. But one look into those sinister reptilian eyes, and you knew—there was no greater predator who stalked the night in Miru's realm.

The other players were the typical rabble the death god kept around. One was a tall, muscular biker type who had a face like a bat, with a scrunched up nose and huge ears on either side of his head. Another was short and thin, in an All Blacks hoodie that the creature had pulled up to obscure its face. Its hands were gray and skeletal, its fingernails black and hooked, and wisps of shadow hung all around it like tobacco smoke. The final player was a patupaiarehe, one of the fae who had long inhabited Maori lands and parts of our underworld. She was tall and lanky in tight jeans and worn black combat boots, with skin as pale as the white t-shirt she wore tucked in at the waist, contrasting with her long, reddish-blonde hair and blue eyes that shone in the dark.

The others were minor gods, representations of illness and disease more than likely. Miru liked those types. But the faery—that was the one I needed to worry about. You couldn't trust the fae, no matter where they were from. Plus, if she was here, she was evil and certainly a powerful sorceress—else Miru's buddies would have killed her already. Maori black magic was nothing to be trifled with, not if a person could help it, and even the gods feared it. I'd keep one eye on her at all times for sure.

The game they played was a combination of pool and a traditional Maori game known as tī rākau. In the traditional game, players tossed sticks back and forth to one another to a rhythm they drummed on the floor and sticks as they played. But in Miru's version, each player held a pool cue they used to tap out a blistering cadence on the floor and edge of the pool table between shots. It was mesmerizing, to say the least.

I stood back and observed, curious regarding how this might play out.

When they tossed their pool cues to each other, whoever was behind the cue ball had to make a shot and sink a ball without losing the tempo or dropping their cue. This was more than difficult; it was nearly impossible, since they had to make a shot in the split-second time gap between beats. No mortal could pull it off, but it was a perfect game for gods and dark creatures of the underworld.

I stood in silence, not wanting to risk the wrath of Miru

by interrupting the game or breaking a player's concentration. I was sure they'd laid some wager on the outcome of their match. High-stakes, almost certainly. So, I waited to the side, silently observing until the game was finished.

It was entertaining, to see these four creatures of dark magic tapping and turning and spinning and beating their cues on the floor. In a flash they'd toss them to one another, and one of the four would sink a ball in a pocket with a shot that would make any pool shark jealous. It was superhumanly impressive and supernaturally hypnotic. Were it not for the divine blood that coursed through my veins, I'm sure I would've fallen under the spell the players wove as they completed their game.

Soon, they were down to one last ball on the table. The pool cues beat out a rhythm and meter that no human percussionist could match, faster and faster as the sticks whirled and blurred. Finally, they passed their sticks, and the faery sorceress was behind the cue ball, directly across the table from me. She locked eyes with me, and without skipping a beat, she sunk the eight ball in the side pocket nearest were I stood next to the entrance.

This, of course, drew all eyes to me as the game ended. The bat god let out a small hiss, while the shadow creature's eyes glowed a pestilent green as they narrowed at me. The sorceress flashed me a wicked smile as she rested the butt of her cue on the floor. I had no idea what that was about, but at least none of the others saw it. That might mark me as her agent or ally, and put me at odds with the other players. Gods were a capricious bunch—

even the so-called good ones—and you never wanted to get on their bad side.

Which was why I was fairly nervous as Miru stared silently at me from the near side of the pool table.

Finally, the dark god smiled, his androgynous features softening while his eyes remained hard. He tsked and spoke in a soft, sibilant voice, his gaze chilling me to my soul.

"Tāwhere, Mutu, Mākutu... allow me to introduce Hemi Waara—Hine-nui-te-pō's son."

24

I observed their reactions while considering the names Miru had spoken. My thoughts lingered on one, specifically. *Mākutu... that's bad, really bad.* I must've given something away in my expression, 'cause her face split in a self-satisfied smirk as she put her pool stick away on the rack. The others just stared.

After I'd put on a stern look, I nodded in Miru's direction, foregoing the more familiar greeting of a hongi. You don't press noses with a god of death—not unless she's your mother. "Miru, just passing through. Came to pay my respects and ask permission for safe passage."

Miru leaned back against the pool table, almost half-sitting as he laid his cue across the felt. "Brave of you, to come back here when I told you never to return. Or stupid. Which is unlikely, since you were never the stupid kind."

I lifted a shoulder slightly, fixing my eyes on Miru but keeping the others in sight. "Had no choice. Died and got sent here by mistake."

Miru tilted his head back and laughed out loud at the ceiling. "By mistake? No one gets sent here by mistake, you know that. Still, you don't belong here, as anyone can see." He stared more intently at me. "You're missing more than one aspect of yourself, I see. Heard about the one, but not the other. It's a shame either way."

"The second is a recent development," I replied. "Now, I just gotta get to my mother's realm so she can set me right. If you'll allow me passage, of course." Tāwhere, the bat god, and Mutu, the shadowy fellow, were whispering and snickering to each other off to the side. I turned and gave them a deliberate look. "Oi, is something funny?"

The big biker with the bat face spoke in a voice that was way too high for his stature. "Just noticed, you got no moko. Mutu guesses you lost it in a bet, but I say someone took it."

My moko, or the absence of it, was a sore spot with me. To a Maori, facial tattoos signify more than just status. They also speak of their history and lineage, telling the story of who they are and *why* they are. My step-dad had managed to steal mine from me, which put him on the outs with my mum, but he'd done it anyway. Who would have thought a guy who spends all his time underground could be such a pain?

"Everybody knows what happened," Mākutu said. "Give it a rest, Tāwhere."

The bat-faced god turned on her. "You mind your own business, witch. The *boy* and I are having a chat, and I want to hear what happened from him." He placed an emphasis on "boy." Now he was really pissing me off.

Miru crossed his arms and watched this exchange with interest, seemingly unwilling to get in the middle of it. I locked eyes with him for a second, and a twitch of an eyebrow told me he wouldn't interfere. Scratching my nose to hide the fact that I was mumbling a spell, I triggered the tattoos on my shoulders and arms. A blue glow lit the dark room up as my mother's magic activated, causing Mutu to shy away. My mum might have been a goddess of the underworld, but she was born up above, and her magic reflects that. For a creature of the underworld, that's something to be feared.

"Still got these," I said with a yawn. "If you can take them, I'll tell you what happened. My side of the story, anyway."

Tāwhere looked like he might take me up on it, then he grinned, flashing a mouth full of needle-sharp teeth. "I'm just giving you grief, kid. Relax."

"Grief, you reckon? As if looking at that ugly mug of yours isn't grief enough."

The bat god glowered at me. "I'll not have you speak to me that way, boy."

"I'll speak to you any way I like. Since you seem set on insulting me, I don't see anything wrong in taking a similar tone. By the way, your face looks like a bag of hammered assholes."

Tāwhere's face contorted with rage, and he let out a screech that sent a spike of agony through my skull. I shook it off just in time to see him launch himself across the room at me, his leather jacket morphing into a pair of bat-like wings.

It was the reaction I'd hoped for, and I was ready for it. Being a spirit now, I'd not be able to interact with stuff around me in the real world. But here in the underworld, I was as substantial as everything here. And as Tāwhere flew at me, I grabbed a pool cue from the wall, holding it with my right hand at the butt and my left near the center.

The bat-faced god thought I would swing it at him, but instead I used it as a spear, shoving the narrow end of it into his mouth and out the back of his head. Then I pivoted, letting Tāwhere's body pass me as I thrust the tip of the pool cue into the wall of Miru's parlor. Since his brainstem was damaged, all Tāwhere could do is dangle there, looking furious and choking on his own blood.

I turned to Mutu. "You want to know how I lost my moko?"

The shadowy god hissed. "No. Ssss-alright. I'm good."

Miru uncrossed his arms and stood. "Well, that settles that. I appreciate that you didn't smash the place up."

I shrugged. "I felt bad about the last time. Didn't want to do a repeat and hack you off more."

The death god rubbed his chin as he looked at me. "Hmm, you've matured somewhat since I saw you last." He considered me for a moment. "You may pass through my realm, but I won't give you any assistance. Whiro and I have always been on good terms, so I won't interfere in whatever he has planned for you. Still, I don't see any reason to anger your mother, either."

"I appreciate it, Miru."

The death god smiled with little warmth. "Oh, don't thank me yet. The path to your mother's realm is hardly clear. Just because I'm not standing in your way doesn't mean something else won't." He tilted his head as if listening to a voice coming from far, far away. "I've business to attend. Please, see yourself out."

Miru vanished in a puff of sulphur and smoke, leaving me to exchange an awkward silence with his guests.

Mutu broke the silence with a hiss. "Anyone up for another game? Winner gets Tāwhere's jacket."

25

I declined Mutu's offer. Playing games of chance or skill with gods, even minor gods, was always a bad idea. Mākutu, the incarnation of witchcraft herself, also demurred. Just as well. Would've been awkward if she hadn't, and I worried more about offending her than playing against Mutu.

Rather than go through the bar again, I decided to sneak out the back door of the place. As I did, I stopped by the kitchen to grab a sharp knife from the rack. Obviously, I hadn't arrived in the underworld armed, so I figured it wouldn't hurt to have a blade on me. Plus, I could use it to carve a *taiaha* or a *tewhatewha* just as soon as I found some wood to work with.

Once I was outside, I took a moment to find my bearings. I had a long way to go before I could get back to my mum's house. First, I had to get through Uranga-o-te-Rā, where Rohe lived—a right nasty character if ever there was one. Likes to devour souls and practices black magic. She was once Maui's wife, and doesn't care for me since my mum killed her husband.

Maui. What an idiot that guy was.

Once I got past Rohe, I'd be in Whiro's territory. Of course, Whiro had it in for me. Or rather, for my corpse, which hopefully was headed to New Zealand on a plane with Colin at the moment. Time was weird in the underworld just like it was in Underhill, so who the hell knew how long I'd been down here? Still, time tended to move more slowly here, so I figured Colin would have my body waiting for me long before I made it to Te Reinga.

No doubt, Whiro had left some surprises for me—things to hinder my passage through his realm. I imagined they would involve monsters, demons, and the like. Fun times. Nothing like a good fight to get a spirit ready to re-enter the world of the living.

After I'd determined the correct direction to Rohe's realm, I headed for a twisted path that led off into the distance. The path soon began to gain elevation as I neared the mountains that marked the boundary between Miru's lands and Rohe's. Just when I'd made it to the foothills, I rounded a large boulder to find Mākutu waiting for me, her pale white skin and fiery red hair providing a stark contrast to the ledge of lava rock she sat upon.

She is attractive, I'll give her that. But poison often comes wrapped in pretty paper.

I stopped and waited, since she was sitting directly along the path and kind of in my way. Not that I couldn't have squeezed by her, but I didn't care to get that close without knowing what she was on about.

I nodded in her direction. "Goddess of witchcraft, huh?"

"Just a practitioner of the arts. No more, no less. As are you, I see. You and I are not so very different, Hemi Waara."

She smiled, displaying perfect white teeth that set off her dark, tattooed lips. The tattoos on my shoulders and arms tingled as they activated, and I suddenly noticed her moko dancing patterns on her chin as she spoke. *Witchcraft.* She was using magic to make her words sound sweeter to my ears. *Tricky, tricky.*

"Hey now, there's no need for that," I said. "I can hear you just fine without the spell craft."

Mākutu's eyes widened slightly, and her cheeks flushed a bit. *Interesting.* "Apologies. It's merely a habit," she said. "Purely unintentional."

I crossed my arms and scratched an itch that wasn't there. "Uh huh. Why don't you tell me why you're here and what you want from me? I've got somewhere to be, so make it quick."

The witch raised her hands, showing me her palms. "I bear you no ill will, warrior. Certainly I don't care to suffer the wrath of your mother, and I'd not underestimate your own skill and power either."

I yawned and rubbed my nose. "You already did, but go on."

Her expression darkened for a moment, but then she smiled again and her displeasure vanished. "As you know, you'll have to face Rohe, which I'm sure you'll manage. However, Whiro has left a powerful taniwha guarding the path through his realm. That one will not let you pass so easily as Miru did."

"A taniwha, eh? I take it the path leads through a lake or over a river of some sort?"

She nodded. "It does."

"And am I to assume that's the only way through Whiro's realm?"

Mākutu nodded again. "You're smarter than you look."

"I hate water monsters." I sighed and rubbed the back of my neck, exhaling heavily. "Alright, what's your game, witch?"

She smiled like someone who knew they'd just gotten the better end of a deal. "It's simple. I help you defeat the taniwha, and when you get back to the realm of humans, you help me get there as well."

I waved my hands back and forth. "Nah, get lost. No way in hell I'm unleashing you on the people of Earth. Who knows what mischief you'd cause, or who you'd hurt once you got there? Besides, we have enough trouble with the fae who're there already."

The goddess of witchcraft pursed her lips in a pout and tsked. "Now, Hemi, really—what sort of trouble could be caused by little old me?"

"The black sorcery kind, that's what. You know my mum still has a thing for humans, right? And that she doesn't take kindly to gods and monsters who want to hurt them? I'd say if you want to stay off her bad side, you should abandon whatever plans you have to cause trouble for her people."

"Who says I'm going to cause trouble for *her* people?

Or anyone, for that matter?" She stretched, striking an intentionally sexual pose. "I'm simply tired of living down here, and I'd like to experience modern life on Earth for a change. Maybe enjoy a little peace and quiet, get a nice little place of my own in the city. Can't a girl dream, after all?"

"And which city might that be?"

"Does it matter?" She swept her arms in a broad circle around her. "I just want to get out of here."

I grunted and scratched my head. Like most fae, she couldn't lie—but she wasn't exactly telling the truth, either. Still, I was alone in hostile territory, I had no weapons to speak of, and I'd soon have to face off with a goddess of no small power and a water monster the size of a Whataburger. My mum likely had no idea I was here, since she would be upstairs waiting for Colin to deliver my body. Maori gods didn't normally like to travel far from their seat of power, and Mum was no exception.

Nope, no help was coming.

"Alright, tell me what I get out of all this."

A broad smile split her face, but her bright blue eyes were serpent's slits as she spoke. "Why, Hemi, I'm going to help you get your ta moko back."

26

We were climbing down the other side of the mountain range, a surprisingly hard thing to do considering that I was a spirit. The trail was rocky and steep, the footing treacherous, and the drop below daunting, since we were more or less descending a cliff face. Recent events had made me leery of heights, so I took my time picking my way down the path despite the witch's impatience.

"I could just fly us down, you know," Mākutu said as she hopped, goat-like, from one ledge and outcropping to another.

"I know, you told me. And I said if you could do that, why not simply portal me to my mum's lands?"

"As I explained, I can't."

"You said, but you didn't explain," I grunted, sliding off a ledge on my stomach. I hung by my fingertips and dropped the five feet or so to the next narrow landing.

"Saying what isn't the same as saying *why*. And avoiding the latter is dissembling, in my book."

"Let's just say I was punished and leave it at that," she muttered saltily.

"I take it that's why you need my help getting to Earth. Figures."

She stared at me from her perch, squatting on a rocky spire that had split from the cliffside, the tip no bigger than the palm of my hand. By rights, she should have fallen long ago. I presumed she was using magic to ease her descent. I refused to rely on black sorcery for such a menial task.

"Yes, that's why," she spat. "Now, could we just drop it? Anyway, we're here."

She leapt off the cliff, and I tried to avoid noticing her shapely figure as she slowly floated to the ground thirty feet below. Although the fae were known to be supernaturally attractive, she was a sorceress. Meaning, it could all be a glamour.

Besides, I had no business being attracted to an evil goddess. I watched her float to the ground just the same, if only to ensure she made it there safely. Then, I clambered the rest of the way down. When I arrived at the bottom, I found her sitting on a boulder, ankle crossed over one knee and slumped with her chin propped on one hand.

"If you'd have let me use my magic to help, we'd have arrived hours ago," she groused.

I wiped my hands on my trousers. "Eh, I'd rather do things the old-fashioned way. Although, you'd think as a spirit I'd be able to fly or something."

She hung her head, cracking her neck from side to side before standing up and stretching languidly. "Doesn't work that way. If anything, it's harder here for spirits than it is for living creatures."

"Huh. Wonder why that is?"

She looked at me as if I were purposely being dense, which I was. "Because the gods like to punish mortals, that's why. This isn't heaven, after all."

I ignored her snappy retort and her attitude. It was beneath a man to waste energy making another person's problems your own. Mākutu wasn't unhappy because of what had been done to her; she was unhappy because of who she was. No one could fool with black sorcery for long and not succumb to the cloud of misery that surrounded it. And Mākutu *was* black sorcery, through and through—that much was clear.

However, I was beginning to think she wasn't evil. That might seem like a contradiction, since I said before that black magic is purely evil. But I got the feeling that she'd once sought power as a means to an end, and ended up being consumed by it. Perhaps I was right and perhaps not. But if so, she wouldn't be the first human or faery to experience a dark transfiguration born from magic. Nor would she be the first to ascend to godhood for it... or *descend*, in her case.

Still, even if she wasn't purely evil, she couldn't be trusted.

I looked off into the distance, where the black night of Miru's lands gave way to the gray twilight of Rohe's realm.

"You're right, we're here." I turned to address her directly. "Are you going to help with Rohe?"

The witch shook her head once. "No, you won't require my assistance with her. She fears you, although she won't say it. She'll send another to deal with you, that you can be certain of—so be ready. When you need me, I'll be there."

Mākutu then disappeared in a cloud of sooty ash and poisonous gas.

"As expected," I whispered.

The gods never liked to get their hands dirty, if they could help it. That was why they so often chose to act through intermediaries. Avatars. Demigods. Sorcerers. Champions. Or any other puppet they could manipulate. I'd learned not to trust the gods while living among them. It had been a hard lesson.

Dealing with Rohe wouldn't be easy. I was in her lands, and she was a notoriously foul-tempered goddess. Once a beautiful woman, her ugly husband Maui had tricked her into trading faces with him. After it was done, he'd refused to trade back. What a prick, eh?

In shame and anger, she'd retreated to the underworld and started devouring souls, probably in hopes of finding a face as beautiful as her own once was. I know it doesn't make sense, but she's one of the gods, after all. They don't have to make sense—no one has to make sense when they have that much power.

Off in the distance, a flock of ravens circled in the air where smoke rose from a large gray *wharepuni*, or sleeping house. I figured that was where I'd find Rohe. I could try to avoid her, sure—but chances were good she already knew I was here.

"Stuff it. Might as well get this over with."

I spotted a path in the rocks and rubble of the foothills, and headed for the smoke and ravens.

27

The wharepuni was immense, a fact that became clear the closer I got to it. Even stranger, the place was made of stone, built from gray basalt in the traditional style of my people. Which was weird, because the Maori weren't known to build their homes from stone. Wood, yes —rocks, not so much.

I had pretty sharp vision, being a demigod and all, so I searched the building carefully for clues regarding how it was constructed. You never knew when a bit of knowledge or insight might come in handy, and it paid to be observant around gods. I didn't see a seam or joint in the entire wharepuni. It was as if it had been carved from a single, giant piece of rock—just the sort of thing a god or goddess would do to show off.

The front door was enormous, easily half-again my height. It stood open just a crack, perhaps to let light in because the interior was dark as night. I detected no movement from the sleeping house, nor from the sparse trees and vegetation around the place. It could have been a dead thing, abandoned and long disused, except for the smoke coming from the chimney.

"Hello the house!" I called.

Silence.

"I said—"

"I heard you the first time!" came the shrill reply. "Knew you were out there since you left the mountains with that sorceress. Not that she'd show her face around here."

"I presume I'm speaking with Rohe, the goddess of the underworld and ruler of this realm?"

She cackled. It was a low, mean sound. "*A* goddess of the underworld, you mean. Not *the* goddess. Couldn't upset your dear old mum, now could you, son of Hine-nui-te-pō? Tell me, is she still as fair as she was the day she fucked her own father? And do the teeth in her twat still gnash together at the memory of my husband's passage?"

I gritted my teeth, capping my temper for the moment. When folks spoke ill of my mother, it got under my skin. Besides my dad, my mum's the only person who ever stood up for me, even in the face of her current husband's fury. Well, her and Colin.

Avoiding a fight with Rohe was tops on my list at the moment, because the longer it took me to get back to my body, the longer it would take to recover. Still, I wasn't about to let her comments go unanswered.

"She's as fair as the day her father raped her, yes. You know that gods never age, as you also know that legend about how she killed Maui is made up. He tried to gain immortality by aping Tāne's trespass, and Mum isn't one to suffer the same indignity twice."

"You lie!" the voice screeched from inside the wharepuni. "Maui might've been a lying trickster, but he was no rapist. He only sought to take what should have rightfully been his as a birthright, had not Makeatutara fucked it up."

Was being the key word in that exchange. As a demigod, Maui might have come back from a simple death. But when a goddess of the underworld kills you, you tend to stay dead. Which is why you don't want to get on Mum's bad side.

And why I didn't want to be on Rohe's bad side, either.

I extended my hands in an attempt to calm her. "Now, now. We could argue all day and night and still not agree on this matter, but that will get us nowhere. I mean no disrespect, and only wish to pass through your lands *peacefully* and be done with it. So I ask you, Rohe—may I pass?"

She chuckled, and it was almost a growl. "You think I care about what your mother did to Maui? Or that he's dead? I'd be thanking her for killing him, except for one small detail—one seemingly inconsequential fact that slipped your mother's mind in the heat of her anger."

The doors burst open, slamming against the front wall of the wharepuni, and Rohe shambled out of the darkness. She was wrapped in rags that had once been bright and colorful garments. Her hair was unkempt and crawling with lice and other vermin, and she clutched a short walking stick in one hand, leaning on it heavily as she moved. Although her form was bent and her stature hunched, I could tell that once, long ago, she'd possessed a shapely figure that must've turned heads for days.

Something's very wrong here. Her arms were still trim and well-muscled, her skin still smooth and unblemished where it was exposed through the holes and tears in her clothing. Her hips were full and curved, and her breasts high and firm, at least from what I could tell under those tatters of cloth. But her face—

Maui must've been one ugly bastard, because Rohe's features weren't just hideous; they were impossible. The structure of her face was like an Escher done in flesh, with lines and curves and mismatched perspectives that caused an irrepressible revulsion on seeing the sum of its parts. What should have been straight was twisted. What should have been symmetrical was imbalanced, and what should have been fine was rough and misshapen.

I was certain that a mortal would have gone mad at the sight of Rohe's unfortunate-looking mug, and I myself nearly retched reflexively. However, demigods are made of sterner stuff, so I managed to maintain my composure a moment before looking away.

"Look at me! Look at what your mother has done! Can you retrieve something that has rotted away, been eaten by worms, and returned to the earth? No, you cannot. And so, I'll forever be cursed to bear my late husband's repulsive, monstrous face. All because the Great Woman of Night couldn't see fit to show mercy—not to him, but for the one whose beauty he stole. Because of her, what was mine is lost forever!"

I forced myself to look back again, swallowing bile as I

locked eyes with poor, unfortunate Rohe. I pitied her then, although I knew I shouldn't. She'd allowed her misfortune to consume her, turning her into a thing that knew only misery. Now, she chose to visit that misery on others.

It wasn't her face that made her a monster, but her choices.

I saw it then, the evidence of her dark deeds. Things crawled under her skin, faces pressing against the surface of her flesh—souls trapped forever inside of her that she'd devoured against my mother's wishes. Yet none of them had sufficed to replace what she'd lost, so she'd continue to eat the souls of the dead who crossed her realm—perhaps for all eternity.

"Yes, I've lost much due to your mother's temper." She smiled at me with her impossibly crooked mouth, leering with her hideous, malformed eyes. "But you've a pretty face, boy. Yes, a pretty face indeed."

Gulp.

28

I backed away from the doors of the wharepuni, keeping one eye in the general direction of Rohe and the other on my escape route. It's not that I feared fighting her—I still had my mother's magic, after all—but I feared the consequences of losing. How Rohe thought she'd take my face off my spirit was a mystery to me, but the gods were known to make the impossible mundane.

Knowing the gods, she probably possessed some magic talent or spell that would allow her to rip my face off my spirit, replacing it with her own. Sure, if I survived I might still make it back to my body. But who wants to live knowing when you die you'll be uglier than a hemorrhoid on a rat's ass in the afterlife?

I figured she probably couldn't run too fast, all hunched over like that. But when I eyed the path that ran beyond her home, Rohe cackled like a mad hen.

"Think to outrun me, eh, boy? You could, true. But thankfully I don't have to chase you down. Do I, son?"

Her eyes looked beyond and behind me. Could've been a trick, but the rumbling noise in the distance and ground-shaking footsteps that approached said otherwise.

Son... what son? I turned to look, and that's when I put two and two together. *Ah, piss. Rangi-hore.*

Rangi-hore was the god of rocks and stones. Which, of course, explained how Rohe's wharepuni had been built. I had to hand it to the guy for taking care of his mum, but I wasn't about to let him beat me to a pulp so she could steal my face. And this fella could definitely beat me to shreds if I let him.

Remember that guy from the *Thor* movie who talked like a bouncer from a K Road club? Well, Rangi-hore didn't look anything like him. I mean, you'd think he would, right? But Rohe's son was even more messed up than that fellow.

The god of rocks and stones was about four meters tall, give or take a few centimeters, and made entirely of rocks. Now, when I say made of rock, I don't mean rock shaped like a man or a guy with stone skin like the Thing. Nope. I mean boulders that were stacked up, one on top of another, in a vague outline of a giant.

I looked up at him and grinned, even as the bottom fell out of my stomach. "Don't tell me... it's clobberin' time?"

"The crow should know it's not safe to caw from the falcon's perch, little one," Rangi-hore rumbled. His voice sounded like scree tumbling down a steep, rocky slope. "Yield, or I'll crush you into pulp."

"I'll have to remember that one, about the crow and the falcon. Good line. But see, I've got places to be, bodies to reclaim, and people to resurrect. Namely, me. So no, I'm not going to yield."

Rohe's screeching voice echoed from the front porch of her sleeping lodge. "I want his face, son—his face! Smash the rest of him to bits, but don't hurt what's mine."

I spared her a glance out of sheer displeasure. "Yours? I'll have you know, I was born with this mug. It's not my fault you let Maui trick you into trading yours away."

Rohe's disgusting face contorted into a rictus of rage and hate. "Kill him! Kill him now!"

I dove to one side, not needing to look to know that Rangi-hore was on the move. A hand that was literally a ton of rocks crashed to the earth where I'd been standing a split-second before. Rather than turn and fight, I wisely rolled to my feet and took off at a sprint toward Whiro's lands and, hopefully, freedom.

As I mentioned before, space and time worked differently in the underworld than it did up in the realm of living humans. I always thought it was because the gods tinkered with the laws of physics so they could torture humans at their leisure. Never got a straight answer from my mum about that, which told me I was probably right.

Anyway, if I ran for Whiro's realm, I had a fifty-fifty chance of hitting a rip in time that would take me there before Rangi-hore could catch up with me. It was kind of like stepping on one of those conveyor belts they had at airports. You still moved at the same rate of speed, but everything around you just kind of passed you by faster.

Of course, I still had to beat the big pile of rubble in the short stretch. He was bigger than me, sure, and he had a longer stride. But I also had the blood of gods in me, plus I had tricks of my own. I could put on the speed when I needed to. I muttered a few spells as I ran, causing my tattoos to glow as Mum's magic flowed through me. Although I'd heard the giant's footfalls getting closer as I fled, I now heard them receding into the distance.

I looked back to gauge my lead—big mistake. Oh, Rangi-hore was pretty far behind me, alright. But when I turned back around, it was just in time to see Rohe's cane as it clotheslined me across the chest. My feet flew up and I flipped upside down, the force of the blow sending me backwards, heels over head.

I landed flat on my face with the wind knocked out of me, along with all the piss and vinegar I'd been full of moments before. I shouldn't have been surprised at what Rohe was capable of, what with her being a goddess and all. Still, it was a shock to see that she could move that fast, not to mention that she packed such a wallop.

She danced a little jig nearby, waving her cane in the air as she celebrated taking me down a notch. "Thought you'd get away, did you? Hah! Old Rohe still has a few tricks. Now, just wait until my boy gets here—he'll make minced meat out of you, and then I'll be wearing that pretty skin of yours."

She was so caught up in her little victory dance she didn't see me recovering. While she was still distracted, I spun around and swept her feet out from under her. As she fell, I snatched her cane away and landed on top of her with the knife I'd stolen from Miru's bar at her throat.

About then, Rangi-hore came up on us. I let the edge

of my blade draw a thin red line over his mum's carotid, angling my arm so he could see. The god of rocks and stone came to a grinding halt several yards away. If a boulder could give a look of concern, Rangi-hore's big stony visage was doing exactly that.

I fixed him with a grim smile. "Bro, I reckon we should sort something out, eh?"

29

"Nice how you handled Rohe and her son back there." Mākutu had shown up again, appearing out of nowhere after I'd dealt with those two crazies. "I was worried you'd try to fight your way through. That would have gone poorly for you, I think—even with your mother's magic."

"Meh," I grunted, swiping another curl of wood away with the knife. I'd held on to Rohe's cane, and was carving it into a war club as we walked. It might have looked like a worn old piece of wood, but it had been in the possession of a god for who knew how long. Thus, it held power—magical potential that merely needed to be shaped and focused. I hummed a tune my mother had taught me as I worked the wood.

"Seriously, Hemi, there's more to you than meets the eye." Her eyes darted my way and back again, almost too fast to notice.

Sneaking glances. What's the deal with this woman?

Suddenly, the trees parted ahead and I surveyed the terrain before us. We were coming up on Whiro's domain, where the gray, stony lands and sparse forests of Rohe's realm gave way to dank, misty swamps and wetlands that comprised much of the god of evil's home. The place was infested with whanau-akaaka, or repulsive ones. Giant insects that could rip your arm off, massive carnivorous reptiles, and carrion birds the size of a Cessna—definitely not friendly territory.

I glanced at the witch and shrugged. "Not every problem requires a hammer."

She nodded as a playful smile split her ink-stained lips. "Can't take down a mountain with a sledge, either—no matter how hard you swing. Anyway, it was well played, Hemi. I'm impressed."

"Is this the part where you tell me I'm not as dumb as I look?"

"No, not at all. I learned a long time ago that it's a mistake to judge people by their appearances. Besides, that old trope of the big dumb guy rarely rings true. I just thought I should give credit where credit is due."

"I know you're buttering me up, Mākutu. Like a hog being fattened up for slaughter, I think."

She giggled like a schoolgirl, covering her mouth as she looked at me with hooded eyes. "Now, Hemi, I'd never hurt you. You're my ticket out of here, after all."

"Don't remind me," I replied as I scanned the trail ahead. We were passing into Whiro's turf now. "I already regret this deal, and we haven't even gotten to the hard part yet. Speaking of which, how are you going to get me my moko back?"

The sorceress' eyes narrowed, the sly smile she constantly wore never leaving her lips. "Come, I'll show you."

She left the trail, parting the dense blades of *harakeke* that lined the path as she disappeared into the swamp beyond. I hesitated to leave the trail. A person could easily get lost in Whiro's part of the underworld and never find their way back. Or get eaten. That was also a distinct possibility.

A pale white hand reached out from within the tall blades of flax, grabbing my wrist and yanking me along. "Come on, there's nothing to fear here. You have my word."

"The word of a sorceress," I muttered as I allowed myself to be dragged into the dense vegetation. The plant life soon parted, giving way to another narrower path that hadn't been visible from the main thoroughfare. Once she'd led me a ways down the new path, Mākutu stopped and turned on me. We were nearly chest to chest, and she craned her neck to fix me with a hard stare.

"Pay attention, god-man, because I'm only going to say this once. *I. Never. Asked. For. This.* So, give it a rest already, eh?"

"This?" I asked, wanting to make sure I understood her meaning.

She took a step back and swept her hands down the length of her figure. "This. Immortality. 'Mākutu, the incarnation of witchcraft and sorcery.' I was mortal once, you know. Not human, but as mortal as a faery being can be. I've been wronged by the gods, just like you have. We're on the same side, Hemi Waara. You have to believe me."

I rubbed my nose with the back of my hand. "How'd it happen—I mean, how'd you get the job, so to speak?"

Her gaze trailed off to the side. "I don't want to discuss it. Just know that I'm not who you think I am, just like you're not the big dumb lug everyone thinks you are."

Hmm, that cut to the quick. Not being judgmental at all, eh, Hemi? "Fair enough." I sighed. "I can't believe I'm saying this to the goddess of black magic, but sorry for being such a prick."

"Eh, forget it already. We have to get moving, so just drop it and we'll pretend it never happened."

She turned away and marched off down the trail. If I didn't know any better, I'd have said she was wiping her eyes as she walked off. *Probably just my imagination.*

"Where are we headed, anyway?" I asked. Although nothing appeared to be out of the ordinary, I could sense we were traveling a great distance in a short period of time. *The path's a warp, for sure.*

"The place I'm taking you was once my home," Mākutu replied over her shoulder. "We'll have to trade with the people who live there for what we need. They kind of live out in the wops, but going there is unavoidable if you want to get back to your mum's. I'm taking us there by way of a shortcut. Even Whiro doesn't know about it."

"Wait a minute—you said they were once your people?"

She moved tall blades of grass aside, parting them with her hands to reveal a fantastic scene beyond, a diorama

146

brought to life. An entire bustling village sprawled out ahead of us, populated by dozens upon dozens of tall, pale, red-headed men, women, and children.

"Yes, that's what I said." She looked back at me, smiling as those cold blue eyes lit up like sapphires in sunlight. "Welcome to the land of the patupaiarehe."

30

Before I knew it, we were in front of the village's *whare runanga*, meeting with the ariki and the kaumatua— the chief and the tribal elders. All the men and women present had the most beautiful, intricate moko on their faces. In the presence of such splendor, I felt quite naked without mine. Upon closer inspection, I realized the style of their tattoos was familiar to me.

They favor unaunahi in their designs, and the ink on their faces dances like Mākutu's. Fish scales in a tattoo design represented health and prosperity, and I'd noticed the same pattern in the witch's ink. Truly, these were her people. But whether she was of them, or they were of her —that remained to be seen.

Another detail I noticed was that none of the men had the pakati, or dog skin cloak design, worked into their tattoos. These people were not warriors, but artisans, farmers, and such. *And, perhaps, magicians.* I recalled how there once lived a people indigenous to the Chatham

Islands who held themselves to a code of non-violence—a peaceful people. The Taranaki iwi, a prominent Maori nation, nearly wiped them out in the 1800s. If Mākutu's people adhered to a similar code, I could only imagine how hard it must have been for them to survive in Whiro's domain.

As the visitor and guest, I walked around the circle, greeting each male elder with a respectful hongi, and the females with a polite hug and kiss on the cheek.

Once introductions had been made and formalities addressed, the ariki spoke first. "Maki says you can help us, Earth-walker."

My eyes darted to Mākutu's, and the tightness around her eyes told me she was trusting me not to rat her out. I glanced back at the chief. "That depends on your problem. But I will help, if I am able."

Mākutu chimed in, speaking with authority. "The tribe faces a dire threat, and unfortunately none of our people have the skills to face it. A great taniwha hunts us, stealing our *wāhine* and raiding our stores of food. This has gone on for some time, and now almost none of our young women are left."

"Except you," I proffered.

The chief nodded. "Maki is very resourceful. She is the one who led us to this place, where we have remained hidden from Waima for a time, in peace. But I fear it will not last."

"Waima," I said. "Offspring of Āraiteuru, the legendary mother of all great sea serpents?"

An elder coughed politely before speaking. "Yes, that

one. These marshy lands are an analog to Punakitere in the world above. Waima, being a supernatural creature, travels back and forth between them at will. We think because it has become harder for him to remain hidden in your world, he prefers the underworld of late."

"And faery flesh, apparently," I countered. "No disrespect intended. Just making sure I understand the situation."

The sorceress clucked her tongue. "In truth, we aren't certain if he's eating the young women he abducts, or simply keeping them for company."

"We hope the latter," a female elder interjected.

The reluctant goddess continued. "Nevertheless, my people are in need of a warrior to face Waima."

I crossed my arms and cradled my chin in one hand. "You want me to kill one of the greatest sea serpents to have ever lived in Aotearoa?"

"Not necessarily kill it," a male elder said. "If you could just chase it away, we'd be happy."

Everyone in the circle nodded in unison.

I sighed. "And just what do I get in return for this monumental task?"

"If you can rid us of this menace, your reward will be in accordance with such a deed." Despite the chief's pretty words, the almost apologetic tone in his voice spoke volumes. In his mind, he was looking at a dead man walking. *Great.* "I am not only our chief, but also serve as our tribe's *tohunga ta moko*. Do this for us, and I will restore your facial tattoos—and imbue them with the magic of my people."

"I dunno," I said, and meant it. "Once Rūaumoko finds out I have my ink back, he'll just burn it off again."

"I assure you, son of Hine-nui-te-po, neither man nor god can remove the markings my hands make," the old faery chief replied. "Moreover, I can make it so he can never harm you in that way again."

"How?"

The sorceress winked at me. "Chief Ue-tonga is Rūaumoko's grandson. He knows the secret to his grandfather's fire—and he can make you immune to it."

That threw me for a loop. I was standing in the presence of the Maori god of tattooing. As my good friend Colin would exclaim at a time like this, *hole-lee shit.*

"Won't that piss your grandad off, you helping me?"

The chief frowned. "He shows little interest in his descendants. Besides, Waima is our primary concern at this time. And if it comes to it, I can deal with Rūaumoko."

I held my tongue for several seconds, mulling the situation over—both what was offered, and what could be lost. The potential gain for me was immeasurable. Once I had my moko restored by Ue-Tonga, my turd of a stepdad could never harm me again. Well, at least not by fire. And that meant he couldn't burn my moko off, which was how he managed to steal it the first time around. *The prick.*

The downside was that I'd be fighting one of the meanest creatures ever to menace land or sea in Aotearoa. Waima was no pushover, that was certain. If I was hesitant to square off with Rangi-hore, I was downright troubled about the prospect of facing Waima.

And if I died now, I'd be gone forever. No coming back

for me, no having Mum resurrect me from the grave, no going back to life as I once knew it.

No more Hemi, period.

I scratched the stubble on my cheek with a yawn.

"Sure, why not? I'm in."

31

Mākutu was ahead of me, deftly picking a path through the swamp. Waima had been searching high and low for the faery village, and subsequently washed out the path in places. Thankfully the sorceress knew the way, and I gladly let her take the lead so I could suss out my strategy. And if I allowed my eyes to wander her way every now and again, I didn't mean any harm by it.

"So, can I expect any assistance at all when I'm fighting this thing?" I asked.

She held a hand up, wobbling it from side to side. "Yes, but it's questionable how much help I'll be. I don't need to tell you what water does to a witch's powers. So long as Waima is partially-submerged, it'll be hard for me to help."

At least Mākutu's people loaned me the tools I needed to finish my weapon.

Rohe's cane had been a straight length of matai roughly five feet long, with a large burled knot on the thicker end. This had made it the perfect piece of stock for a tewhatewha—an axe-shaped, long-handled war club that could be used for bludgeoning or as a stabbing weapon. The night before, I had spent hours polishing it smooth and bringing its surface to a sheen by rubbing shark oil into the wood.

The weapon would do well against most mortal and some supernatural enemies, but it was hardly enough to take down a giant sea serpent. I clucked my tongue and rubbed the war club with my thumb. Like a worry rock, it gave me something to do with my hands so my mind could wander.

As I thought about it more and more, I admitted to myself that I couldn't fight Waima. To do so would be suicide—quick, painful, and permanent.

However, I knew someone who *could* easily take the creature down. "Mākutu, are there any fissure vents or hot springs around here?"

She nodded. "I know of a place. Why?"

"How far is it from the lake where Waima lives?"

She shrugged. "A mile, perhaps."

Perfect. "Okay, here's what we're going to do..."

I STOOD several yards away from the sulfurous, bubbling pools that represented a gateway to Rūamoko's realm. "Rūamoko! Coward! Thief! I got my moko back. Haere mai! Come see if you can burn it off!"

"I hope you know what you're doing," the sorceress whispered from the bushes behind me.

"Ssshh, he'll hear!" I whispered back. "Rūamoko!" I yelled even louder. "God with no honor—face the one you wronged!"

I knew I'd attracted his attention when the ground began to rumble and shake beneath our feet. The hot springs shot up like a geyser, and a face appeared in the steam they left behind. Then, the god of volcanoes and earthquakes spoke.

"Like a piece of shit stuck to my foot, you follow me around like a bad smell." His voice was overwhelmingly loud, a combination of thunder and escaping gasses. "What do you want this time, little half-breed? Isn't it enough that I put you in your place already?"

The ground shook just a bit, causing me to stumble slightly. I caught my balance and laughed. "The joke's on you, Ru. Look!" I pointed at my face. "I got my moko back. And I brought a friend with me, to show you what's what."

The eyes that had appeared in the steam above the pool appeared to squint. "Who gave you those markings? I forbade anyone in my hapū to replace what I took from you. Come closer, so I can burn them off a second time!"

The markings on my face were nothing more than a little of the witch's magic mixed with pine sap and ash, but he wouldn't know that. Rūamoko had notoriously poor eyesight, the result of having to create eyes from steam and lava on the fly whenever he manifested an avatar above-ground. I just hoped the lines Mākutu had painted on my face wouldn't run due to the heat and humidity Ru threw off, or we'd be done for.

Time to put this crazy plan in motion.

"I don't think so, ya' prick. Come see if you can take on my bro Waima! He hooked it up with the ink."

The hot spring exploded in a cloud of steam and gas as my stepfather released a great deal of pent up rage and frustration. It rankled him that he couldn't kill me, so taking my facial tattoos had been the next best thing. And now, for his plans to have been foiled... well... he wasn't exactly known for his calm demeanor in the face of defeat.

I took off at a sprint, hoping that Mākutu was as good as her word and could pull off this next bit well enough to fool Rūamoko. I realized all at once that she could leave me hanging right now and still achieve at least part of her goals. *Please don't let her be that evil.* I felt a bit of magic wash over me, then a mirror image of me went running off toward Waima's lake. *Thank goodness.*

The illusion wouldn't fool Ru if he got too close, but with his poor eyesight he'd never realize he'd been fooled until he was tussling with Waima. As soon as my doppelgänger sprang off into the distance, I took a sharp right and hid in the tall grass of the nearby swamp.

The only sign that Rūamoko followed my twin was a rumbling beneath the ground. It grew louder as Ru approached, gradually petering out as he passed. Thankfully, the god followed the illusory version of me as it led him to Waima's roost.

"Are you sure this is going to work?" the witch asked.

I chuckled. "Trust me, by the time he gets to the lake, he'll be so pissed he'll boil off half the water on his first pass. Once Waima figures out he can't fight a volcano, he'll move on to greener, wetter pastures—or he'll head back up topside and eat some tourists."

We heard a roar in the distance that was distinctly draconian in nature. Taniwha were basically dragonkind, a long-distance cousin to wyverns, basilisks, Asian water dragons, and the like. So, it was easy to tell when my stepdad arrived at Waima's watery abode. I stood up and looked off into the distance, where a cloud of steam was rising above the wetlands. It obscured the view, while at the same time serving as a signal that Rūamoko had taken my challenge to heart.

"Poor Waima," Mākutu said with a giggle. "He must be so confused right now, wondering how he pissed off a greater god."

"Eh, sucks for him. Shouldn't have been abducting maidens and whatnot. You sure they'll be okay, what with Ru making such a fuss?"

She nodded. "If any are alive, they'll be fine. One of the first things Ue-Tonga does for newborn children in the village is protect them from fire. Besides, that old man has been around for a long, long time. Many of the girls are his descendants, and they share a portion of his powers."

The ground suddenly shook, an earthquake that emanated from where Waima's lake used to be. More steam arose in the distance, then a loud screeching roar sounded from afar. The rumbling and roars continued, but they grew farther and farther away with the passage of time.

Once the tumult caused by Rūamoko and Waima had faded into the distance, I nodded in that direction. "Alright, then. Let's see if there are any maidens to rescue, and then we'll go talk an old man about a tattoo."

32

W e'd found many of the tribe's missing *wāhine* on an island that now stood like a mesa in the middle of the dry lake bed Rūamoko had left. Of course, they'd hidden when the fighting began, but when the girls heard Mākutu singing a *Karanga* welcoming them back home, they came right out. Sadly, more than a few of the young women had been eaten. Waima *was* a monster, after all.

Still, I'd earned my reward.

My tattoos took more than a week to apply. Eight grueling days, in fact. I'd heard stories from old-timers about how painful traditional tattooing methods were, but nothing had prepared me for the agony. However, Ue-Tonga was a practiced and skilled tohunga, and he knew how far to push me each day. Just when I thought I could take no more, he'd stop and tell me to rest, and we'd take it up again the next morning.

I spent the remainder of my time among the patupaiarehe doing just that—resting, healing, and enjoying their music, food, and company. Mākutu stayed with me every day, attending to me and using her magic to help heal the chief's work faster. In the evenings, we took long walks, often not speaking or even needing to—instead simply enjoying each other's presence.

After a few days, I realized I was beginning to believe what she'd said. She wasn't at all what I had thought her to be.

Once my ta moko was complete, it was time for me to leave. True to his word, the magic Ue-Tonga had woven into the ink held protection against fire of all kinds, natural and otherwise. If Rūamoko wanted to harm me now, he'd have to find another way to do it. I wondered aloud whether my tattoos would transfer to the body that awaited me aboveground, and the chief assured me the magic would bond with my corporeal skin once my spirit re-entered my body.

The night before I planned to depart, I found myself strolling through the jungle with Mākutu at my side.

"Will you return with me, now that everything's settled?" I asked, trying hard to prevent any eagerness from showing in my voice.

She smiled demurely and looked up to the sky. There were no stars in the underworld, but giant fireflies flew high above, like slow-moving comets crossing the canopy overhead. I'd learned that Mākutu enjoyed watching them. They reminded her of the night sky above Aotearoa.

"No, I can't. Not until you provide the way." She reached into the air, pulling something from a pocket of nothingness. It was a bundle of twigs and grass, wrapped in flax cord. She held it out to me, pulling part of the bundle back to reveal a burning ember deep within.

"What's this for?"

She placed the bundle in my hands, cupping hers over mine. "When you return to your home, light a fire in your hearth using this ember. When you do, it'll provide me the means to cross over into your world once more."

I reluctantly placed the fire bundle into the woven flax *kete* I wore strapped over my shoulder. The village girls had gifted it to me, along with many other fine presents. A few of the girls we'd rescued had suggested showing their appreciation in other ways, but I'd pretended not to notice. My behavior hadn't escaped Mākutu's attention, however, and she'd chided me relentlessly for being shy. Coming from her, I didn't mind being teased so much.

"Mākutu, I—"

"Sshh, you'll ruin it," she said.

Mākutu reached for my hands, grabbing them in hers as she leaned into me. On impulse, I leaned in as well, lowering my head until our foreheads and noses touched.

"You wouldn't have gotten this close to me a week ago," she whispered.

"I didn't know you a week ago," I replied. "Thankfully you didn't turn me into a toad for my rudeness, else I'd never have gotten the opportunity to see who you really are."

She closed her eyes and gently pulled away. "You still haven't seen who I truly am. Not really. Consider that fact on the long journey back to your home."

Ignoring the reticence in her voice, I held on to her hands. "I've seen what I needed to see. I've witnessed how you are with these people, looking after them, and how you've been toward me these last few days. That's all that matters."

Mākutu shook her head. "I have responsibilities, Hemi. There's more to being what I am than who I would like to be."

I thought about it for a moment, about what she was trying to tell me. "You know, I was also brought into being under strange circumstances, and by powers beyond my control. You try being the son of the goddess of night and death, and see how you like it."

She laughed softly. "You were born a demigod. I was cursed with this. It's not the same thing."

"As if being the offspring of a goddess and a mortal isn't a curse. I'm forever caught between two worlds, not fitting completely in either, and always looking over my shoulder for one god or another to do me in. It's no picnic, Maki."

Her thumbs rubbed my palms. "I like it when you call me that."

"It fits."

Blue eyes that sparkled with the light of fireflies looked up at me. "Perhaps we're not so different after all, Hemi Waara."

I leaned in to steal a kiss, and the immortal incarnation of black magic and sorcery didn't bother to stop me.

"Not in any way that matters," I whispered, just before my lips met hers. "Not in any way that matters at all."

This ends *Blood Ties*, a Junkyard Druid urban fantasy short story collection! If you want more urban fantasy mayhem featuring Colin and his friends, visit http://geni.us/colinmccool to check out the complete Colin McCool Junkyard Druid series.

AFTERWORD

No story is written without the help of others, and I certainly wouldn't have completed this collection without outside assistance. As this volume marks the fifteenth fiction title I've released since I wrote *Colin McCool and the Vampire Dwarf* (a.k.a., *Druid Blood*), I figured I'd better recognize a few people who have helped me along the way.

Please note that I've omitted the last names of anyone who isn't a public figure, out of respect for their privacy.

First, thanks go out to Jared Wihongi for sharing the Maori warrior culture with me. I'd also like to thank Tyrell G. for helping me with Hemi's dialogue, and for fact-checking all the mythological details as well. *Whakawhetai ki a kōrua*, gentlemen.

To my editor, Elizabeth B., thank you for fine-tuning my prose, and for helping me deal with my addiction to commas. And thanks to Lori D. for cleaning up my daily output while I was hammering these stories out.

Kudos to my cover designers, Clarissa and Christian, to

my graphic designer Raisa, and to my VA, Nathelle. If I look like a pro, it's due at least in part to their help.

Thanks as well to my readers for supporting me through fifteen books. I'll keep writing them, as long as you keep reading them.

Finally, thanks to my family for supporting my decision to become a fiction author. You're my whole reason for doing this, and don't you ever forget it.

Of course, any mistakes in this book are my own, and when asked I will *always* blame it on the whiskey.

~M.D. Massey

Made in United States
Orlando, FL
09 March 2022